Welcome to the Modern World, Charlie

Michael Anthony Adams, Jr.

SIX SEEDS PRESS
Baltimore, MD

ISBN: 978-1-952240-05-8

Also by Michael Anthony Adams, Jr. and Published by Six Seeds Press

Fiction:

The Adversary's Good News: A Novel
Psychedelicizations: Short Stories
The American Apocalypse: Short Stories
Crossroads Blues: A Novel
The Cars Behind, Beside Us: Short Stories
Welcome to the Modern World, Charlie: Short Stories
Notes from the Idle Mind: Short Stories

Nonfiction:

Disorder: An Avant-Garde Memoir of Psychosis, Healing and Love

Poetry:

We Are the Underground: Poems
From Now to You: Haiku
Recipe for a Future Theogony: Poems
Indigo Glow: Poems
The Tree Outside My Window: Poems
At the Side of the Road: Poems
Soundtrack for the New Millennium: A Poem

www.6SeedsPress.com

Welcome to the Modern World, Charlie

For Collomia Charles

Contents

Welcome to the Modern World, Charlie

Welcome to the Modern World, Charlie

Charlie swung his door closed. A rattling crash reverberated through the house. Having made his point, he dragged his feet across his stained carpet to plop onto his bed. Lying there, rigidly still, he tightened his already taut features a little bit more. He almost screamed, but instead, biting his lip, he slammed his fist into the mattress.

The room was still for a moment. Charlie closed his eyes. A breezeless warmth burned through the open window above his bed. The sticky, Southern air pasted itself onto everything in the room. The disheveled dresser was sweating against the wall opposite him. Littering the floor, crisp socks and shorts and tee shirts grew moist again. Even around Charlie, the damp air thickened. A busy fly buzzed past his ear. Charlie opened his eyes to gaze up at the crack in the ceiling above him.

For a moment, he thought that if he looked hard enough, the one crack might splinter into a thousand cracks that would expand into a million cracks. Then, letting him gaze at both a topaz sky that he could escape into and a golden sun that he could fly to, the entire ceiling would disappear. But when reality reduced the limitless heavens back to a single, dark imperfection in the white paint, Charlie sat up.

Dangling his spindly legs over the side of the bed, he hung his head. Tiny mounds of dirty clothes rose up from the landscape as if they had sprouted from the frayed carpet itself and had remained intertwined with those dismal strands. Charlie followed the fly's path over a precarious road of stained socks to the largest mountain of worn clothing.

The fly settled onto a flat, white, square corner of something peeking out from beneath a pair of grass-stained shorts at the bottom of the pile. Like a miner proud of the gold he has discovered, the insect paced back and forth, rubbing its forelimbs together in anticipation of the unearthed jewel.

Wiping away uncried tears, Charlie stood up. He walked over to see what was hidden beneath his clothing. Dropping to his knees and brushing away the fly, he removed the flat square that was as big as his chest.

On the back of the white album sleeve was a black and white cross of four faces. Recognizing them, Charlie smiled. He turned the album over in his hands. The band's name swirled above a splotchy sparse collage of bright colors and other worldly things (a disembodied smile, a butterfly, a dragonfly, a hummingbird...). Beneath the letters' puffy outline was the solid shape of the Roman numeral three. Charlie hugged the album to his chest.

When his dad had still lived with them, this album had been his. Charlie could barely picture being in a nicer house, and he kind of remembered an old, wooden turntable in the den, and he could almost see his dad sliding the black vinyl out of the sleeve, and he thought of the hiss and the crackle of the needle, and he saw himself setting up his action figures on a table, and he remembered his dad sitting in an over-stuffed armchair, and he pictured the music crying at him from the speakers.

And when both his dad and everything his dad owned had disappeared, somehow the record had been left behind. Charlie had taken it into his room. He had spent his days and nights playing with his black lab, Theo, and listening to the sounds hidden inside the record's grooves. It was during one of those nights, long after his mom had gone to sleep, that he decided his dad must have died. If he hadn't, he would have come back for the music he had loved so much.

When the man, Frank, started spending time at the house, the record stayed on Charlie's plastic turntable while he hid in his room. Theo hid from the man as well. One night, with the dog barking and the music playing, Frank came in to ask Charlie if he could keep things a little quieter because he was doing work.

Charlie got angry. With a scratch of the needle, he took the record off. He put it back in its sleeve, and he dropped the sleeve on the floor. In the aftermath of summer, as Charlie and Theo spent their days outside in the grass and the heat and the mosquitoes, he forgot about the record his dad had left behind.

So today, in the midst of the late afternoon heat, when the crack in the ceiling would remain only a crack, Charlie wiped his eyes again. He got off his knees, and he walked over to the little, single component stereo with a turntable on top. Holding the record with one hand, he pressed the power button. A soft "pop" sounded through his messy room. In the speakers beside his dresser, a static noise buzzed.

He slipped the vinyl out of the sleeve, and he twirled it between his fingers. The record caught the light in its grooves, and it shined. Charlie put the record on the turntable, but just when he was ready to press play, his door creaked open.

Charlie spun around.

His mom was in the doorway. She was young and thin with long, blonde hair stringing around her face and dangling across her tee shirt. She quietly clicked the door closed. She walked across the carpet to settle onto the bed. Exhaling, she glanced around the cramped dirty room that she had given Charlie and that Charlie wouldn't have to live in much longer. "I know why you're angry," she said while studying the crack in his ceiling. Then, she turned back to him. "But you're not being fair."

Turning off his stereo, Charlie sat down, Indian style, on his floor. His mom wiped a strand of hair off her face. "We already talked about it," she said. Charlie shrugged. "You know Theo can't come with us," her voice trickled away. "We talked about that…"

Charlie gave another melancholy shrug.

"What do you want us to do?"

"Not move to New Haven."

His mom looked back at the ceiling. "Frank's job is there," she said.

"But why do I have to go? My last name isn't Hammond."

His mom was stunned. She whispered, so that if Frank was walking down the hall he couldn't hear, "It doesn't matter whether or not your last name is Hammond. You're coming too."

"Why?"

"Because you're my son, and I'm not going anywhere without you."

"But why do we have to go anywhere?"

"Because we can't stay here."

"Why can't we stay here?"

His mom laughed sadly. "Look around you, Charlie. Look at this house and this street, and you tell me why we can't stay here."

Charlie didn't answer. Even at his age, he wasn't blind to the dilapidation of the chipped paint both inside and outside their home. Even he understood the degradation of the faded façade of their Southern neighborhood. He picked at the worn carpet. His lower lip began trembling. Trying so hard not to cry, he raised his chin. His mom slid off the bed to join him, cross-legged on the floor.

For a moment, she was on the verge of crying as well. She creased her forehead, and she explained, "Frank really cares about us, Charlie, and he has a better opportunity there than here. We're just lucky that he asked us to come too. This sort of stuff doesn't just happen…"

"But how do you know New Haven will be any better than Athens, Mom?"

"We have to believe it will be."

"Without Theo, it can't."

"Charlie," his mom pleaded, "I wish Theo could come too. Frank wishes Theo could come…"

"Then why'd he give him away?"

"Because we'll be in an apartment, and it's not going to be big enough for a dog the size of Theo. You can't expect him to stay cooped up all day without a yard and without a neighborhood to roam around in."

Charlie didn't answer.

"Maybe, once we get settled there, and we get a house, we can get another dog."

"I don't want another dog."

"Charlie, we don't have a choice…"

But Charlie wasn't listening. Not caring whether or not Frank was close enough to hear, he cried to his mom, "But why'd *he* get to give him away. Theo was my dog. I should have taken him out there. Not him."

"But you said you didn't want to be there…"

"That's because I didn't think you'd do it." He choked on a wad of tears. "I didn't think you'd do that to me."

His mom whispered something. She crawled across the floor to give Charlie a hug and let him cry into her shoulder. She spoke quiet, kind words. She smoothed his hair, and she told him that, soon, everything would be okay.

Charlie sniffled a few times. He whispered, "If Dad was still alive, he never would have gotten rid of Theo."

His mom froze. "What did you say?"

"I said that if Dad was still alive…"

His mom pulled away from him. She said, "Charlie, your dad's not dead."

A slight spasm dried Charlie's eyes. He'd been on his knees when his mom had hugged him, but now he retreated into a more guarded pose. He had never told her about his dad. He figured that she already knew and that, for some reason, she was hiding the truth from him.

"Who told you your dad was dead?"

Charlie tightened his jaw. He squeezed out the name, "Nobody."

"Then why'd you…" His mom brought her fingers up to her mouth. "Charlie," she began, nervously fidgeting with her lips over every carefully chosen word, "Your dad left. He didn't die."

"Then why hasn't he come back?"

"I don't know. I don't even know why he left." His mom knew that was the wrong answer, but she didn't know what else to say right then. She shook her head, and she stood up. "I'll come check on you later," she whispered, and she left Charlie alone in his room.

Charlie sat still in the silence. The humidity had sucked the air from his room to leave him drowning in its moisture. A tear dripped down his cheek, but he didn't sob. He didn't even wipe the single tear away. He just sat there, wishing he could hear Theo bark.

He wished that if he closed his eyes, when he opened them, the black lab would be shining like the record had in the sunlight. Theo would open his dark, droopy jowls for one deep, friendly sound, and Charlie could crawl on his knees to be smothered from hair to chin in the wet laps of the dog's droopy tongue.

But Theo was gone now, too. Frank had given him away that morning. The man had put Theo in the backseat of a car, and he had driven the dog, who, the whole way, had whined and scratched at the window, to a farm. Frank said that Theo would be able to play there when the rest of the family left Athens next week. Charlie had stayed in his room until Frank had come back. When Theo hadn't come back with him, he'd yelled. With a rattling crash, he'd slammed his bedroom door.

But when that had happened, he'd thought his dad was dead. He'd thought that it had to be that his mom was crying and that there was some man named Frank to care for them. But his dad wasn't dead. That meant none of this made any sense.

Another fly, or maybe the same fly, buzzed past Charlie. The slight noise startled him back into his bedroom's filthy heat. Taking a moment to wipe the sticky tears from his cheeks and chin, he watched the fly zoom lazy circles around his room. Once again reminding him of what he had forgotten, it landed on the stereo.

Charlie walked over to the turntable. He pressed power again. With another quiet "pop", the speakers buzzed into life. The fly rubbed its hands. The little arm swung its half arc to land on the record's grooves. Being written by the needle's bobs, the album hiss climbed to a song. Charlie walked back to his bed.

The music struck the jarring, violent melody that his

dad had loved so much. Charlie landed on his mattress. Looking at the single, thin crack above him, his eyes filled with tears. Now, even more than before, he needed that crack to engulf the entire ceiling. He needed the walls to cave down without a ceiling to support them, but when a voice's high-pitched cry wailed above the music, everything beyond the moment of sound disappeared.

The fly flew silently. Thoughts of Theo disappeared into the rhythm. Trapped inside the record, the voice wailed in another dimension. It cried to Charlie from that otherworld where the inhabitants were his overlords, and Charlie thought that, maybe, he might have been there, once, a long time ago.

The Albatross

Only one person made it on the bus before Jay. Her name was Skye, and in her crisp, new outfit, she glided up the aisle to slide into the single seat that Jay had wanted for himself. Over the summer, Skye's blonde hair had grown longer and wavier, her complexion had smoothed and soaked in a deep tan, and her thirteen year old body had sleekened and matured in preparation for turning fourteen and entering the eighth grade. To Jay, however, she was still a skinny, quietly stuck-up girl – just like she was last year – who had taken the seat he already had warned everybody was his.

Reaching the emergency exit, he scowled at her, but she didn't see that. Grunting, he plopped into the double seat across the narrow aisle from her, and he propped his empty backpack in place beside himself. It was the first day of eighth grade for him too, and now, he was just another overweight kid drowning in his ill-fitting tee shirt and his baggy jeans. He picked at a piece of silver electrical tape bandaging one of the wounds the bus had received from so many middle school children's pens and pencils. He frowned, closed his eyes, and snuggled his cheek against the window on his left.

Outside the bus, the sun had recently risen. The neighborhood's brick and wood-sided homes wallowed in the early morning's muted colors. As the bus climbed up and dropped below the suburban hills, the road ran on through the next four stops. At each one, the older kids, the ones in Jay's and Skye's grade, muscled their ways as far back as they could get, while the younger kids, glancing at the back, waiting for when they would sit back there, filed up the steps to sit wherever they could. The middle school voices filled the bus with a roar of both summer stories and complaints about the coming day.

With a subtle screech of the brakes, the bus stopped again. Jay's cheek smeared across the glass. The door at the front jerked open. Another mob of tired and excited children stepped into the narrow aisle. Jay scooted up in his seat. He dropped his pack to the floor. With an anticipatory nod, he indicated the empty space beside himself. Accepting the invitation, the kid that he had been waiting to see smiled.

The bus sailed on again. Damien sat down beside Jay. "Whuz up, Cuz?" he asked.

Jay shook his head, "Nothin'."

Yawning and rubbing his hands across his cheeks, Damien glanced at Skye. Struck by something, he snorted a short laugh. Scooting to the edge of his seat, leaning down to the same level as Jay, he smiled and whispered, "Thought you were gonna sit over there," and he jerked his head back at Skye.

Jay narrowed his eyes. "I was gonna."

Damien spat another short chuckle. He looked down on his left and shook his head.

Beneath the gaze again, Jay fidgeted with his shirt. Sweating slightly, he whispered, "What's it matter to you? It's not like you haven't been sittin' back here since we were in sixth grade."

Damien nodded, "And I'm back here no matter who's sittin' where you are," he reminded his almost friendless friend.

Jay frowned.

"How'd she get on before you?" Damien asked.

Jay shrugged.

Changing the sound of his voice, Damien waved his arms excitedly, "I'm the man at Southside Middle. Nobody fucks with *me* there. Everybody knows I'm the man," he burst into a cheeky laughter while Jay gazed up scornfully and scraped his feet across the pink and yellow remnants of chewing gum on the floor. With a high, drawn out wheeze, Damien stopped laughing long enough to look to his right.

Skye crossed her legs at her knees. She tried stretching her skirt's sheer fabric farther down, but she couldn't cover any more of her legs. Deaf to the conversation beside her, she stared at the trees zooming past her reflection in the glass.

Damien's laughter echoed above the noisy bus. "Yo," he jabbed, "You better hope all those little kids know it's not like you didn't *let* her sit over there."

Jay glared at the girl who had taken the seat that, a couple days before, he had bragged would finally be his. "They know," he told his friend, but when he picked at the electrical tape again, his acne covered face turned scarlet.

Jay peeled up a sticky corner of tape. It left a milky white residue beside the edge of the seat's puffed out hollow scar. He pulled then smoothed the loosened flap that stuck and stretched both to and from the cushion's smooth skin. From the corner of his eye, Damien watched Skye absent-mindedly fold and unfold her short skirt's tiny hem. He swung his arms to settle himself in his seat. He perked his eyebrows up in an arc. An almost unnoticeable smile touched the corner of his lips, but Jay was too enthralled with trying to touch the scar on the seat to notice. Then, the bus stopped again.

Jay quit playing with the tape. He turned to Damien who glanced down at him. Both boys turned toward the front. The doors collapsed open.

"Added a stop," Damien noticed. Unlike everybody else, unimpressed by the prospect of a stranger, he returned his hidden glance to Skye. But the unexpected stop broke even her trance. Flicking her neck, she turned away from the glass.

A tiny pause echoed through the bus. A slender, blond boy stepped up the steps from the curb. His face was turned to the rubber mat on the ground. He paused at the end of his short climb. He stared at the kids, and they all stared back at him.

Motionless and silent at the entrance, Chris twitched his features. He tugged at his empty backpack's loose straps. He passed his gaze across the uneven heads of the kids sitting shoulder to shoulder in their seats. Swerving his eyes from the left to the right, he unblinkingly met the faces of the boys and the girls. Far away, at the very end of the narrow aisle, he saw Skye.

For less than a second, she held her breath. Her gaze locked onto Chris's. She smiled. A tiny grin spread across Chris's face, and he looked back down.

Following Skye's smile with his panic-stricken gaze, Damien watched the entire momentary exchange. He collapsed deeper into his fake leather seat. His tight jaw went slack beneath his stunned eyes, and his face lost the color that Chris's gained.

"You know anybody'd moved here?" Jay whispered.

"Uh-uh," Damien murmured uneasily.

The bus lurched toward the school. Chris stumbled forward. Losing interest in the new arrival, the kids' voices continued their self-absorbed shouts of glee and protest. Chris took off his backpack, sat down in the empty seat directly behind the driver, and slid all the way across to the window.

He pressed his fingers against the glass, and he whispered to his reflection, "She smiled at me." Grinning, he fell into a daydream about watching her smile at him every day.

Damien glared at the back of the blond boy's head. He looked down at his own black hands clasped on his lap. Frowning, he moved them to the seat where he could bury them beneath the extra fabric of his jeans.

Still slouching beneath the weight of his clothes, Jay still picked at the tape. He grimaced while struggling with the bus's bandages. For the first time since the last stop, Damien tried laughing nonchalantly when he said to him, "You see that new kid checkin' out Skye?"

Looking up from the tape, Jay glanced questioningly at Damien. He turned to the front of the bus. He turned back to glare at Skye. Scowling at his friend, he shook his head.

"It's just funny, you know, he'll get schooled by a stuck up bitch like her."

Jay whispered, "Fuck her."

Damien laughed a quick laugh.

Eventually, the bus pulled into the school. With a unanimous groan, all the kids stood up.

Chris stretched from his seat. He tried sneaking one last glimpse at the girl who had smiled at him before he had to leave with nothing other than her memory to propel him through his first day in that unfamiliar place.

Skye stood up. She ran her hand through her hair. She gazed at the front. She caught Chris's eye right before he stepped down into the crowd. They left each other with another exchange of smiles.

Damien stood still for a moment. Breathing deeply, he flared his nostrils. He raised his head high, and he muscled his way into the crowd.

Jay was the last to leave the bus. He didn't even notice his friend get up. All alone, frowning at and playing with the tape, he sat still in the back. Then, gathering his courage, he labored to lift himself from the seat. He walked down the aisle to step off the bus to be lost, while struggling with his ill-fitting clothes, among the raucous throng.

When Jay climbed back up its narrow steps that afternoon, the bus was as still as a library. For a moment, the metal and glass formed a shell sealing him away from the noise of the outside world. In the silence, he thought he might be the only one aboard. Exhaling his tensely held breath, he turned to walk to the very back, but Skye was still sitting in that single seat. She leaned forward and smoothed her skirt. It was as if she hadn't left her place over the course of the entire day, but Jay knew she had. During English class, he'd talked about her with Chris, the new kid. In Math, he'd thought about what Chris had said. And when he saw her again in History, it kind of made sense.

He carried his heavy backpack to the same seat he'd had to sit in earlier. He slid over to the window. He wiped the sweat off his forehead. Struggling to make himself more comfortable, he lifted his arms to air out his pits. Skye didn't notice him. She was staring at the crowd surging toward the bus. But the sight of her in the silence was enough to convince Jay that Chris had been right, and he was able to relax.

Then, the moment was gone. The noise of a thousand screaming middle school kids broke on the bus. Jay came to attention. From amid the turbulent mass, Damien appeared and glided to the back. He slid into place beside Jay. He looked at Skye, and he laughed, "You still over here?"

Jay shrugged.

"The way you were runnin'. I figured you had to beat her this time." His voice gained a fevered quality. Running in place, he pumped his arms and gasped between deep breaths, "I'm gonna make it... I'm gonna make it this time." To keep himself from choking on his laughter, he wheezed and slapped his chest.

The bus was filling up. Jay started picking at the tape.

"Yo, Cuz," Damien screwed up his nose. "You *musta* been runnin'... You reek!" and laughter exploded from him once again.

Jay sniffed the air. He lifted and dropped his shoulders, and he went back to peeling and pressing the tape. The tape popped off the seat, and Jay ran one hand along the long-ago-made scar. With the other hand, he balled the tape into an adhesive mass, and he began playing with another one of the bus's bandages.

"Whatcha doin' with that?" Damien asked him.

"Dunno."

"Lemme see it."

Jay threw the tiny ball into the air. It revolved on its awkward axis, twirled to change its shade in the window light, spun a downward arc, and landed in Damien's hand. He tossed the balled up bandage back into the light and the air. Up and down, up and down, Damien threw himself short, pop flies. He caught them all, and every once in a while, he glanced over to see if Skye was looking. Jay bobbed his head along with the ball, and every once in a while, he looked too, to see if maybe Skye had turned to him.

A frail, white hand appeared on the seatback in front of them. A new voice sounded above the bus's roar, "What's up, Jay?"

Damien closed his hands around the semi-sticky ball. This time, he didn't open them again. He dropped his hands into his lap.

The new kid pulled at his ear and rearranged the straps of his heavily stuffed backpack. Damien grew rigid in his seat. Jay responded, "Nothin'. What's up?"

With a tremor, the bus joined its voice to those of its occupants, but the back was silent. Chris shook his head.

A spasm passed down the bus line. When it reached the bus that Chris was standing on, he floundered, slipped, and tipped toward Jay and Damien.

Jay leaned back into his seat. Damien thrust out his hand, with the tape stuck to his palm, to keep Chris from falling on them. A giggle came from across the aisle. Flushed and clutching the seatback, Chris swallowed and glanced at Skye. Amid a flurry of her hair, she turned back to the window.

Damien started breathing again. He dropped his hand to hide it in his tee shirt's folds.

Growing more embarrassed by the moment, Chris whispered, "See ya." He turned, walked forward two seats, glanced to the back, and sat down next to some kid who he didn't know at all.

"See ya," Jay said.

The bus rolled away from Southside Middle. The kids laughed and shouted and made fun of each other. Claps and slaps added percussion to the melody. Silently, a pen dropped to the ground. When the bus changed gears, it rolled between the freely swinging and the nervously shifting feet to the back where it bumped into Damien's shoes. He leaned down and picked it up off the floor.

Jabbing the pen into the tape ball, he asked Jay, "What's up with him?"

Jay lifted his shoulders. "He's all right," he murmured

while picking at the newly triangularly peeled edge of his most recent piece of tape.

Flaring his nostrils and clenching his jaw, Damien tried spinning his own makeshift sphere on the pen's axis. It twirled then stuck, twirled then stuck. Leaving a dark, gaping hole in its semi-solid surface, he pulled out the pen. "What's his name," he asked.

"Chris," Jay responded, "And you know what? He does like Skye."

"How you know that?"

Jay succeeded in ripping the other bandage off the seat. He smiled and ran his finger along the milky goo it left behind. "He told me she looks like some actress his dad likes."

Damien laughed so hard he stomped his feet on the ground. "Her?" he shook his head.

"No, I know who he's talkin' about, she kinda does."

Damien popped the pen into the seat. "Gimme that," he said. He grabbed the loosely flapping tape from Jay's chubby fingers. Trying to make a better ball, he wrapped it, sticky side out, around the sphere he held. "You think he's right?"

Jay didn't answer. He lightly flicked the pen sticking out of the seat. It wobbled like a knife in the ground.

Damien laughed, "So what's up with that?"

"I dunno," Jay said. He turned red and felt sweat creep into his armpits.

"You think you could get with her?"

A single drop of sweat slipped from a pore and ran down his ribs.

"When she straight up makes you look like a chump?"

Jay shrugged and struggled beneath the weight of his clothes.

The bus's noise brightened as the school disappeared.

Closer to the front, Chris shook his head, thinking, *Jeez, that looked smooth.* The kid next to him struggled to become more comfortable in his seat. Chris glanced at the quiet, dark haired kid leaning against the window. He wanted to say something to that kid, to introduce himself, but he didn't even know where to begin. *He's not like Jay*, he thought, and he remembered how the fat kid had sought out an awkward friendship when the two of them were next to each other in English.

I can't believe he never noticed her. He turned to sneak a peek at Skye. Her hair was thrown across her opposite shoulder. The same sun that was warming her lit her neck and nose and lips. She blinked. Letting her eye wander toward him, she lifted her eyelash. Still embarrassed at being caught mesmerized, Chris turned away, but he didn't notice the other sets of eyes watching him from behind pointed fingers.

Skye... he mused, and he smiled. *She does look like her*, he assured himself. Comfortably settling onto the edge of his seat, he scooted down and let his foot fall into the aisle.

Jay seemed all right, he thought, and he flew into a daydream about a not too distant time when he could hear Skye talk, when she would smile with every word, when he would never turn red and look away simply because there would be no reason to. Jay was part of the daydream too. He was Chris's good friend. He kept telling the new kid about how everybody was awed at where he had come from that had made it possible for Skye to like him. Because, just like Jay had complained about her earlier that day, she never talked to anybody.

The harsh scraping of feet walking along the bus's rubber mat embellished the noise. Chris heard it, but he didn't pay any attention to it. A soft slap, leaving behind a light weight, landed on top of his head. Dragged from his dream to his seat, Chris reached up to feel what had crowned him. He tried pulling off the sticky mass, but as he struggled, he intertwined his hair with the gluey crown, and it was quickly stuck.

He pulled at the tape that pulled at his hair that pulled at his face, but nothing happened. He turned to see who had done this to him. Sliding into place in the very back, struggling quickly to get overtop of Damien, Jay was framed by the window. Laughing and covering his mouth, Damien was pointing at Chris. Smiling himself, Jay sat down. Damien slapped him five. And then Jay saw Chris staring at him.

Chris left his hand still on the tape. The kid next to him lifted his head from the window and snorted a short laugh. Chris crashed back into his seat. He scooted down and tried struggling, below the seatback where nobody could see him, with his crown. The same tape was bandaging the seatback in front of him, and Chris realized that he would never pull it out of his hair.

Dropping his hand, he silently cried, *I thought you were gonna be my friend.*

The bus screamed to a stop, and its doors groaned open. Chris grew rigid. Putting his hands on either side, he lifted himself from his place.

From the back, a burst of cheeky laughter greeted his face. Like popcorn, the laughter exploded all around him. It leaped from the open mouths behind their pointing fingers, bounded across the seats, sprang over the aisle, bounced from window to window, ricocheted off the walls and ceiling, and slammed into his head. Reflecting in the rectangular, rearview mirror, even the bus driver's fat face stared at him. He stood still while the happy voices lashed and stuck him from every side. He grabbed his backpack off the seat. Turning to the ground, trying not to see anybody, he hurried through the narrow aisle. The heavy crown weighted his downturned head, and that only made him more comical and more absurd, and that only made the bus roar harder.

The windows' shafts of sunlight spilt across his path. Chris passed from patches of green darkness through the sun's rays. His lips quivered, his forehead was creased, he was sniffling, and the bus's nameless, faceless jeers assaulted him from either side.

He struck something with his shin. His arms flailed through the air. His head rushed toward the ground, but he caught himself right before his face struck the sticky floor. He turned to see what had happened. A laughing mouth, gaping like a black hole, rocked back and forth while its hand slapped the knee of the leg that was still stuck in the aisle. Chris started running.

Behind him, a boy with a shaved head leaped from his seat to flail his arms in a mocking mimicry of Chris's fall. That kid then collapsed in a fit of laughter back into his place.

Finally, Chris reached the end of the aisle. Ready to fling himself off the bus, he spread his arms and grabbed either side of the open doors, but right before he leaped, he glanced to the back of the bus. Even Skye was stifling her giggles.

Why'd you do this? Chris thought. Holding his breath, he plunged off the steps. The doors closed behind him.

The bus rolled off again. The laughter continued for a moment. Then, as if the new kid had never been there, it was absorbed back into the put downs and curses.

In the back, though, Damien was still laughing. He looked across the aisle and caught Skye's eye.

"That was funny," he said.

Skye leaned into the light shining from the back down

the aisle. Her lip curled up in a grin. "It was mean," she whispered.

"But it was funny," Damien responded, leaning, with his own grin, into the light.

Skye's face was only a few inches from Damien's. He could smell the fruity scent of the shampoo that she must have used hours ago. She smiled embarrassedly and nodded her head. Giggling, she moved back into her seat.

Feeling his cheeks surge with color, Damien nudged his bony elbow into Jay's ribs. "Told you it'd be funny," he said.

Jay didn't answer. He didn't even look at Damien. He pulled his shoulders up to hide himself in the clothes that he was making look bigger than they already were. He grabbed the pen that Damien had left sticking out of the seat. He pulled it down. With a rough noise, the hole ripped into a gash that bled a bit of cottony stuffing. Jay shifted uncomfortably. He tried taking a deep breath, but his chest felt too heavy.

Attempting the Night

The wave rolled back into the silhouette of a face laughing in the darkness before it leapt forward to rage against the shore. A screaming rattle of broken shells cried out beneath the foam and the spittle, and they were dragged, clawing the sand, bleating like a thousand sacrificial sheep, to their abysmal graves, when the ocean inhaled a breath of earthen air.

The moonlight highlighted the water's undulations. It traced a barnacle-crusted pier's rickety shape in the distance. It brushed across the dunes. And it gave shadows to Ike and Lucas. The diamond shapes of their surfboards loomed behind them. Their feet were dusted by the sand their footprints had replaced. Their seats were shallow indentations in the sloping beach.

"Shore looks differ'nt," Lucas drawled. He wrapped his arms around his legs.

"Yeah it does," Ike said.

Running his hands through the sticky tangles of his salt-spiked hair, Lucas looked at the pier. The distant shapes of the fishermen flinging their lines behind their heads were emblazoned on the darkness by the pier's misty lights. The fishermen were staring over the railing, slapping each other's shoulders, and lifting beers to their mouths. Lucas nodded at them, "Ho-Daddies' out e'en t'night," he said.

Narrowing his eyes, Ike looked over his shoulder, "Yeah," he whispered, "Probably chummin' for Old Nick."

"You think Ol' Nick'll be out t'night?"

"Naw… They're probably just tryin' to bring him in from wherever he's hidin'."

Lucas nodded.

Another wave wracked the shore. The earth screamed and disappeared beneath its foaming jaws. Clouds flew across the moon. For a moment, the entire world was black. A jagged wire electrified the sky, and the beach glowed. A few seconds later, thunder buried the ocean's noise.

"Don't think they're comin'," Ike said.

Lucas frowned and nodded. "I know."

Ike stood up. He brushed the sand from his hands and legs. Lucas did the same. They pulled their surfboards out of the ground, set them on the beach, and wrapped the rubber leashes' velcro straps around their ankles. Picking up and holding his board under his arm, Ike smiled at Lucas, "Ready?"

Lucas brushed the sand off his board's nose. "Let's go."

They screamed as they ran down the beach.

On the pier, a few of the fishermen looked up from where their almost invisible lines poked through the water's surface. One of them took off his faded cap and wiped the sweat from his forehead. He shook his head at the two surfers charging the raging waves, and he mumbled something about how somebody better be home by the time he was. With his callused hands, he grabbed a plastic bucket filled with chopped up fish heads and tails, and he dumped the thick mess over the side of the pier. The bloody spew splashed in the water, and the ocean gurgled and swallowed the chum.

The pattering thuds of Ike's and Lucas's feet sounded

down the beach. The sand stopped caving in beneath them. It grew wet and hard. They slapped the earth into quickly dissolving, muddy footprints. Then the ocean licked their toes, lapped their ankles, slammed into their shins, and dragged against their knees. They leaped out of the water and threw their boards in front of themselves.

Slicing through the air, the smooth, glassed decks reflected the moon. Ike and Lucas, with the ocean dripping off their leg hairs, flew over the shore break and splashed onto the choppy water. The boards dipped slightly beneath their weight, and a layer of soapy salt slid across the decks.

Lucas shook a few drops of water from his face. Grinning, he licked his salt flavored lips. He pulled his arms back and over his head to propel himself away from the shore, away from the sand, away from the suck and pull of the bound currents, and toward the sandbar where the ocean formed into the waves that pummeled the beach.

The Atlantic surged beneath him. It bucked his surfboard. It tugged at the three fins guiding him through the water. It swelled and shook on either side. Lucas used his chest, his back, his shoulders, his entire body to strain against the current. He splashed over the tiny white caps. All around him, the world was a churning, writhing black mass highlighted here and there by the spitting gasps of tiny breaking waves. He stopped paddling and held the nose of his board as the ocean's backdraft rushed him over the smaller waves, and he started paddling again.

Suddenly, the water deepened into a gorge. A smooth force propelled him into the trough. The world rushed past his ears. He stopped paddling and looked up. The ocean was flexed into a frothing wave blocking the entire sky. Lucas held his breath. He brought his knees onto the board, and he used all of his strength to plunge nose first into the water, to try and dive to the shelf of land buried underneath the ocean's surface.

In the daytime, the ocean was a window of quicksilver running around children's legs and bathers' bodies. The line-up of surfers paddled and splashed and laughed far beyond the people crowding the shore. The waves barely reached the chests of the boyfriends and girlfriends who leaped into the sea's white-tipped embrace. Beneath a never-ending chorus of seagulls, sandcastles cooked and hardened beside the babies' buckets that had built them. Parents reclined in chairs and used their sunglasses and hands to shade their eyes.

Two girls whose legs were thin and bronzed and whose bathing suits were tight and curved and whose hair draped off their shoulders and across their towels lay on their backs. Wiping water from his nose and carrying his surfboard under his arm, Lucas nodded at them when he told Ike that he needed to go talk to somebody.

Ike smiled at his friend trudging up the sand. By the time he reached the girls, the conversation had already started.

"...We jus' thought y'all might wanna learn how to surf," Lucas was saying. He was crouching next to the girls, smiling unevenly, and watching beads of water drip off his shorts and pelt the sand.

One of the girls, cupping a few drops of sweat in her smoothly folding stomach, rose on her elbows. She bent one shining, oiled leg. She giggled, whipped her hair across her neck, and asked, "And why did you think that?"

Lucas smiled. He glanced over his shoulder at Ike standing behind him. Then, he looked back at the girl who was sitting up, the girl in the blue bikini, the girl he'd told Ike he was going for – Ike could have the other one. A spattering of freckles dotted her nose. Her eyes were as blue as the ocean he'd just left. Her smile was full and straight. The scent of her coconut flavored suntan lotion was enthralling and invigorating. For a second, Lucas couldn't remember what he wanted to say. He shook his head, and he laughed, "Cuz ev'r'body wants to surf."

The other girl, the one who was still lying down, the one with black hair and a black bathing suit that clung to her bigger breasts and that was cut high above her shorter legs turned toward him. She squinted and shaded her eyes, "You think so?"

Lucas glanced at her. "O' course," he smiled. He turned back to the other girl, "What all else y'all gonna do at the beach?"

The girl who was sitting up laughed, "Right. What else are we gonna do?" Her friend lying in the sand just pursed her lips, settled a pair of sunglasses across her nose, and let the light caress her body.

"What were your names again?" the girl in blue asked. A coy expression thread through her lips and eyes.

Lucas lit up brighter than the glowing beach. "I'm Lucas an' this here's Ike."

The girl in blue laughed. She looked at her friend who grinned and wrinkled her nose. "Nice to meet you Ike and Lucas. I'm Michelle and this is Gabby." She put out her hand.

Grabbing it with his, Lucas felt warmer than the summer water he'd just left. Gabby struggled onto her elbows. Ike planted his surfboard in the ground and sat down at the girls' feet.

"Now why should *you* guys be the ones who teach us how to surf?" Michelle asked.

Lucas closed his eyes and wiped one of his shaking hands across his face, pulling the last remnants of water from his cheeks and sliding a grin onto his lips, "'Cause me an' Ike 're the bes' surf'rs in all o' Car'lina Beach."

"'All o' Car'lina Beach'..." Gabby repeated, and she laughed.

Lucas narrowed his eyes, "Wha'd you say?" He was turning as red as most of the tourists.

Ike bent his head and laughed quietly. Both of the girls watched his chiseled shoulders rise and fall with his chuckles.

Gabby leaned her head back. She rubbed her hair against her shoulder blades. She let the sun soak into her pores. "I just never expected a surfer to have an accent like yours," she said.

Ike's quiet chuckles overflowed in a burst of laughter, "Jesus, what *did* you expect? He lives right over the bridge."

"In that trailer park?" Gabby asked.

Ike turned his lips up in a half grin. He nodded. Lucas looked back over his shoulder. He clenched his fists.

"Where are y'all from?" Ike asked

"Richmond," Gabby answered.

"And you've never been to Carolina Beach?"

Gabby smiled derisively. She shook her head.

"Well, Jesus, it's not like y'all are in California," Ike laughed. He curled his lips and deepened his voice to mimic Lucas's drawl, "For Chris'sake, my daddy's got a Confed'rate flag hangin' off the front o' our house. An' ev'ry mornin' he gets up an' wants me to sing Dixie 'long with 'im 'fore I grab my board outta one o' the Fords that're jacked up in our front yard." Ike shook his head in mock disbelief.

Michelle dropped her eyes. She giggled. Gabby wrinkled her nose, "You keep your surfboard in a jacked up truck?" she asked.

Ike stretched out. He relaxed onto his elbows. His washboard stomach tightened into thick folds. He laughed,

"Naw, I made that part up. We don't have any Fords. And my dad doesn't make me sing Dixie, and we don't even have a Confederate flag." He was quiet for a moment. Then he pointed at Lucas and said, "*His* ho-daddy old man's the one whose been flyin' a flag, waitin' for the South to rise again. Isn't that right, Luke?"

Lucas looked up. Ike was smiling at him. He wiped his nose and looked at the ground. "Yeah," he whispered.

"So when are you going to teach us how to surf?" Michelle asked.

Lucas looked at her. "When you wanna learn?" he asked, but he didn't sound like he believed her.

"I don't know," Michelle leaned toward him, "We don't know anything about it yet."

The breeze mingled the scents of her hair with her skin. Lucas dropped down from his crouch to sit on the beach. He ran his hand through his hair. The salt in it left it sticking up straight. "It's the mos' 'mazin' thing in the whole worl'," he said.

Michelle's eyes glassed over a little bit. "Why's that?" she asked.

"'Cause once you're in the wat'r ev'r'thin' dis'ppears. It doe'n't matt'r where you come from. It doe'n't matter where you been. All that mattr's 's the ocean an' the wave an' wheth'r not you can ride it."

Ike smiled, "Sometimes it's like your whole life never existed."

Gabby buried her feet in the sand at the end of her towel. She scrunched up her face, "How's that?"

"'Cause you're there, and you're paddlin', and the next thing you know, the wave catches you, and if you're lucky you'll be able to bend down and it'll break right over top of you." Ike sat back up. He curved his hand upside down to show the wave's curl funneling over a surfer. "And once you're in that barrel, the whole world's silent. All you hear is the water rushin' over your head. And there's this little point of light at the end, and everything's pushin' you closer and closer to it, and just when it seems like you'll never get there, it's like the whole earth crashes behind you, and you fly back out into the world."

"And that happens every time?" Gabby asked.

"Naw…" Lucas frowned. "Not 'n the Atlantic. You gotta go to Cal'fornia or Hawaii for that to a'ways happ'n."

"You've been to California?" Michelle asked.

"Not yet," Ike said, "But I'm takin' Luke with me next time I go." He smiled at Lucas.

Checking her tan line, Gabby picked one of her bathing suit's straps off her shoulder. "How'd you get to California?" she asked.

"Ike's spons'red by Perfecshun," Lucas told her.

"What's that?" Gabby asked. Satisfied with her tan, she leaned forward to brush a few gains of stray sand from her leg.

Ike squinted through the sunlight. "Just this local shaper." He glanced at Michelle. "They flew me out there for some contests a while back."

Gabby stopped in the middle of brushing sand from her calves. She smiled at Ike. "They fly you anywhere else?"

"Florida… And they're supposed to be sendin' me to Hawaii soon."

"Ike's gonna go all over the whole worl' surfin'," Lucas said. He looked down at the saturated sand around his legs.

"Are you sponsored?" Michelle asked.

"Naw," Lucas frowned, and he twirled his fingers through the grains around his toes. Michelle watched him.

Nobody said anything for a little bit.

"Do you ever have like fish or anything swim into you when you're out there?" Gabby asked, running her feet through the sand, bulldozing it into Ike's soles, "Cuz I think that would just be too weird."

Ike laughed, "Y'all would never believe the things that happen out there."

Michelle leaned closer to Ike, "Like what?"

Lucas burst into the conversation, "Well, like this one time, me an' Ike 'ere out in the wat'r, an' I feel somethin' brush 'gainst my leg. So I reach down to grab it an' it winds up bein' the tail o' this sand shark."

"Are you serious?" Gabby asked. She looked at him for the first time since she had made fun of his accent, "What did you do?"

Lucas ignored her. He stared at Michelle as he spoke. "Now, see, if I was jus' some kook I prob'ly woulda tweaked an' been all like, '*Oh my God! A shark! Whaddo I do now?*' But I spent my whole life 'roun' here. So I jus' sorta lean toward Ike, an' I say, 'Ike, shark in the water,' An' then we stay real still 'til the nex' wave an' once we see it buil'n', we jus' turn 'roun' real slow an' ride it in an' wai' a li'l bit, then go back out. Can't let no shark keep you outta the water."

Michelle was confused. "Really? That's it?"

"I'd be flipped out," Gabby let everybody know.

"Half the time, we don't even bother comin' in," Ike bragged, "We jus' keep surfin'. Sharks don't attack."

"Right," Gabby laughed. Michelle braced herself against the sand, and she giggled.

"There's a shark out there right now," Ike said.

Michelle stared at Ike, "Like a sand shark, right?"

Ike grinned and shook his head, "Nope. Hammerhead."

Gabby froze. She took her sunglasses off. Widening her eyes, she leaned closer to him, "A hammerhead? Are you serious?"

"Yep. I'm serious."

Gabby tried to look like she didn't care that a shark might be swimming beneath her every time she stepped into the water. "Don't they attack people?"

"Maybe," Ike shrugged, "But Old Nick's no big deal."

"Old Nick?" Michelle asked.

"The shark."

"You guys named him?"

"Why not. He comes 'round here every summer."

"*Every* summer?" Gabby couldn't believe it. "Shouldn't they close the beach or something?"

Ike grinned. "He never attacks anybody. He just swims 'round all day and watches. Too many people for him to come close to shore. He'll feed at night though. That's why all those ho-daddies been out on the pier lately. They've been tryin' to catch him for years."

"So you just don't surf in the night?" Michelle asked.

"Naw," Lucas quickly cut in. "Tha's the bes' time."

"Yeah. Me and Luke even talked 'bout goin' out tonight."

"Whaddaya mean talked? We're gonna do it."

Gabby and Michelle looked at Ike.

He shrugged. "Storm's comin' up from the Gulf. Suppose to hit 'round ten. Luke figures he'll get a chance to ride some real waves for a change."

"It ain't for a change. I ridden hurr'cane waves 'fore." He stared at Michelle. "When it gets like that, it don't e'en *look* like the Atlantic."

"If that's your idea of fun," Michelle shrugged.

"What else 'm I gonna do?"

Talking to herself, Gabby twisted her neck a little as she reasoned, "How about *not* go swimming with a shark."

The tourists were filing off the beach, yelling for their children and packing their bags and folding up their chairs to go home and eat dinner, to leave the sand quiet and still like it was on the days when it wasn't summer. Michelle quickly picked a watch up off her towel. Her eyes grew wide when she looked at it. "Gabby, it's after five."

"Are you serious?"

"Yep," Michelle nodded. She turned back to Lucas. She frowned and told him, "We gotta go."

"Why?"

"It's Gabby's dad's birthday tonight. Her family's having a big party for him, and we're supposed to help make dinner."

"Oh," Lucas mumbled. He looked at his feet.

"We'll meet you guys out here tomorrow though," Michelle started telling him, "We'll be out around one or so…"

"How 'bout y'all come out tonight," Ike said. "We'll teach you how to surf then."

Crouching to fold her towel, Gabby smiled, "You're kidding, right?"

Ike shook his head.

"Well how about if we meet you out here after the party?" Michelle asked, "Not to surf, just to hang out." She smiled at Ike. She checked with Gabby who nodded that that was okay with her.

"Sounds good," Ike said, "What time?"

With all her things neatly packed into the towel that she held under her arm, Gabby stood up and told him, "Probably about ten or so."

"We'll be here," Ike smiled.

Michelle smiled back, "All right." She placed an elastic band between her teeth. Closing her eyes, pulling her back in to accentuate her shape, to extend the length of her torso, to outline the curves of her ribs stacking up to her breasts, she slowly ran her hands through her hair to tie it into a ponytail. "Well, it was nice to meet you guys."

"Nice t' meet you, too," Lucas said. He brought his hand up in an embarrassed wave.

"So we'll see y'all tonight?" Ike asked the girls as they started walking away.

Michelle looked over her shoulder at him. She nodded. "Just don't get eaten."

"Ain't happ'ned yet," Lucas answered.

Gabby grinned, "There's always a first time." Michelle slapped her on the shoulder.

Michelle and Gabby struggled up the sand to cross the dunes to walk down the street to the rented condos where Gabby's family was staying. Silently, Ike and Lucas watched them slip away. Their slim calves rose prettily from the sand. Their bronze hamstrings flexed and relaxed at every step. The fabric of their bathing suits jutted out and moved with their muscles. Their backs, easing around their spines, stayed straight and long. Their hair brushed against the skin below their tanned shoulders.

"Man, Ike, if I cou'd get a g'rlfrien' like that, I wou'dn' have to surf."

"Yeah you would."

Lucas frowned and looked at the ground, "Fig'red you'd think some'in' like that."

But the scent of the ocean had already drawn Ike's thoughts away from the girls laughing down the street. "Come on," he said, "Let's go."

Ike and Lucas picked their surfboards up and walked toward the water, to paddle and splash around in the placid, high tide because there was no reason for them to bother going home.

With a jarring smash of white water, the wave crashed above him. The ocean swallowed and choked on itself. As the force pressed him to the ocean's floor, Lucas held tightly onto his surfboard. With every bit of strength he had, he swam below the raging surface that pushed and pulled in every direction.

Unlike when the sun broke through to light the underwater world, everything was black. The salt burned Lucas's eyes. His lungs were about to burst. He struggled beneath the roar. Eventually, as the swirling, bubbling water passed over his head to drag at his feet, he clambered back from the depths.

His board broke free of the water and popped back into the night. Lucas gasped.

A drizzle began. Ike yelled something. Lucas glared at him, but in that same second, he felt the residual tide of the wave that had just crashed above him begin dragging him back to the shore. He gritted his teeth, flipped his sopping hair off his forehead, set his jaw, and strained to free himself from the current.

At first, he was stuck, splashing on the surface. Then, the tide's trembling fingers slipped down his legs and held for a moment to his feet before they disappeared as they ran on to dig into the already battered shore.

The warm wind picked up. It whipped the churning water. Gaining force, the drizzle splashed into the ocean. The second wave in the set rose up. Lucas paddled as hard as he could to reach the giant before it slammed across his back, burying him beneath the water.

White spittle, glowing in the moonlight, dripped from the top of the wave. Lucas closed his eyes and held his breath. Praying that he judged right, that the wave wouldn't break while he was still in the middle of it, he dove into the massive wall of water. He quickly came out on the other side, and the pitch of the plodding wave whined into a run as it rushed to the sand.

Ike laughed. He was sitting on his surfboard, slicking

back his soaking hair, and flexing his muscles. Lucas slid up the length of his board, pushed his chest off the deck, and dangled his legs into the water. The ocean bucked beneath him. It wanted to swallow him.

The third wave in the set began rising. "Wait 'til the last one," Ike shouted.

Lucas nodded, *I know, I know.*

Lightning striped the sky. Seconds later, thunder rumbled across the waves.

"Hah, hah! Whew!" Ike shouted above the sound of the rain on the water. "Your girlfriend shoulda been more worried 'bout us gettin' electrocuted than eaten," he laughed.

Even in the darkness, Lucas smiled in case his friend was watching, but to himself, he whispered, "She'll more likely be your g'rlfrien'."

The fishermen were still on the pier. They hardly even noticed the rain. It did nothing more to them than water down their open beers. Their caps were pulled down tight over their heads. Still looking for Old Nick's fin, they folded the floppy, worn brims to let the rain run onto their cheeks and shoulders.

As the third wave rolled underneath Lucas's board, he squinted through the rain to see if his dad was back there on the pier. He thought he might have seen the old man's hat, but the pier was too far away. The lights igniting it weren't enough to distinguish any more than vague, glowing shapes.

"Here it comes," Ike shouted, "You ready for a real wave!"

With a quick twist of his head, Lucas glanced at Ike, *I been ready f'rever*, he thought, but his palms were sweating in the water.

Out of the night, a huge wave rolled toward them.

Lucas pulled and spurred his board back to the shore. In one quick motion, he scooted down and began to paddle and kick. The tide's backwash reared up behind him and held him stationary. Then, the ocean caught his board, and Lucas was on top of it, looking down at the choppy surface ten feet below him. Beside him, the tip of the wave began dissolving. No longer needing to swim, now being carried along by the ocean's momentum, he grabbed the board's rails. He slid his legs up on the deck, and as the nose of the board dipped down, he stood up.

With a spray of split water trailing behind him, he was flying down the face. Pushing against the board buoyed up by the water, his legs were bent. Unlike earlier, beneath the warm sun, when there was time to think and when he could see what he was doing, he instinctually twisted his torso and pushed down with his left foot, his back foot. He carved back up the smooth face. Reaching the top, he pressed down firmly on the tail of his board, digging its fins into the ocean.

For a moment, he was floating along the edge of the breaking water, slicing through the spilling foam. Then, he twisted even farther. In an avalanche of white water, he fell with his board into the trough. The darkness roared. The wave's warm breath spit on his back. He closed his eyes. Still caught in the rage to reach the shore, he leaned into the foam behind him. The moon lit the white bubbles around his body. The ocean pulled at his shoulders and his arms and his back. Lucas strained his stomach and battled to get back upright. His glistening face reflected the moon, and he smiled as he realized he was still riding the wave.

The darkness started closing in around him. One last time, Lucas spun and cut back up the wave. This time when he reached the lip, he didn't stop. His board flew into the rain and the air. Crying out, Lucas leaped, along with it, into the night. The surfboard landed alone, but he kept flying, spreadeagle above the water. Then, the leash running from his ankle stretched to the limit. He pointed his arms and dove into the ocean.

When he resurfaced and gasped for breath, the soothing rain washed the salt from his eyes. For a moment, the moonlight broke through the clouds. Grinning, Lucas dog paddled through the water. Grabbing hold of the leash, he pulled himself back to his surfboard, struggled onto its deck, and tried to paddle back out before the next set broke.

Out there, Lucas realized that the opposing directions they had gone in and the strength of the tide they had struggled through had separated him from Ike. Ike shouted something above the torrent, but the wind and the rain and the ocean tore his voice apart and scattered it across the water. Lucas didn't care. He smiled and nodded and waved.

He glanced over his shoulder at the beach. Buffeted by the storm, the reeds on the dunes lay flat against the sand. The moonlit beach itself, dissolving beneath the waves and the rain, was so lonely in comparison to the ocean's action. "Maybe Michelle'll come down here soon," Lucas whispered, but as soon as he thought it, he frowned. He didn't want her to come. He didn't want anybody to drag him out of the ocean, away from the waves, off his surfboard on to the hard ground where there was no watery canvas for him to carve – not tonight, not when the Atlantic wasn't the Atlantic, not when he could face and ride the kind of waves that usually only Ike had the chance to ride.

He smiled. Deciding that there was no reason to watch the shore when he could watch the ocean, he squinted through the rain for the next set.

Now that his eyes were used to the night, Lucas noticed

a tiny shape, not too far in front of him, poke through the water. It barely broke the surface, but it sloped backward into a tiny point and dropped straight into the depths. Then, it disappeared.

Lucas's heart started beating faster. He kept his body still, but he turned his head quickly in every direction. The shape surfaced again to his left. Again, it disappeared. *Maybe it's jus' a sand shark*, Lucas thought. *You can't tell how big a fin is from its tip*, he told himself, but he still spun his head around.

The fin popped up again on his right. It looked like it might be a little closer, but it disappeared before he could figure out if that was really the case. "Easy, boy," he whispered. Hoping to see a wave that he could ride, that would take him farther down the beach where he wouldn't have to worry about the fin, he looked in front of himself.

Something looked like it might be forming, but in the darkness and the rain, it was hard to tell where the ocean ended and the sky began. Directly in front of him, definitely closer than it had been, the fin popped out of the water. To Lucas's mind, it rose up at least a foot from the surface. "Oh my God," Lucas breathed. Then, everything but the sharp tip disappeared beneath the roll of a wave. Then, even that disappeared. The ocean barreled toward him. Terrified, Lucas wondered whether or not Old Nick was hidden beneath it. He yelled, "Shark in the water!"

He spun his board back to the shore. From the corner of his eye, he saw Ike nod and wave. Then, he was paddling and kicking as hard as he could, knowing that, at any moment, something might bump the bottom of his board, might chew through the nose, might rip through the flesh in his leg because, to Old Nick, he was just a fish struggling in the water.

The ocean caught him. It roared on every side. It

dropped down what looked like at least twenty feet to the choppy surface. Lucas found himself wondering whether or not Carolina Beach could hold a wave that big. Not even in hurricanes had he seen the ocean so far below him.

The white water walled up and closed out to his right and his left and even behind him. It threw him off the wave. His board shot out from beneath him. Lucas fell forward. The wave spat the tiny stick back into the air, but it held onto Lucas and slammed him against its surface. His ribs slapped the water. In one forced breath, all of the air in his lungs escaped, but the ocean didn't stop. It buried him beneath itself. It slammed his face against the shells on its floor. His surfboard was caught in the retreating tide. Dragging his lips and nose and forehead across the sand, his leash ripped at his ankle.

Choking on salt, trying to free himself, Lucas fumbled with the leash. He ripped the velcro off, and he struggled back to the surface.

His throat and nose and eyes burned. When he was finally able to barely catch his breath, he reached up to wipe the stinging water from his face. His forehead and nose burned like his esophagus. His lips tasted of blood.

Suddenly, he remembered the stories of sharks pinpointing a drop of blood in the water to within a square inch from over a mile away, and Old Nick wasn't that far. Lucas could see the shark swimming through the depths. Intent on his scent, the beast was blind to the raging waves, seeing only the awkward wounded shape. Old Nick was coming straight at him this time. He wasn't bothering to circle. His face was bristling with row upon row of serrated teeth. Guided by the blood in the water, he was going to attack and thrash and rip and tear.

Trying to body surf the shore break, Lucas slapped at the choppy waves. One caught him, buried him in whitewash, and left him behind, struggling, picturing Old Nick writhing toward him. Another wave caught him. It pushed him forward and set his feet on the ground. With his legs shaking, Lucas fought the tide. The backwash tried pushing him back, but he knew that Old Nick could still get him, even if the water only reached his knees, much less his chest.

When he got to the shore, he collapsed. He rolled onto his back and made a snow angel. Melting into the wet sand, he gasped for breath and let the softening rain pelt him. Now he could feel the difference between the warm water and the warmer blood on his face. The salt singed his cuts. His throat and nostrils were on fire. His eyes were bleary and bloodshot from the sand and the sea.

The edge of the ocean licked his feet. A roar shook the earth, but Lucas waited for Ike to slap his shoulder and laugh about how quickly they'd had to run from Old Nick. "You see me ride that wave, Ike?" Lucas would ask. Ike would smile and nod, and tomorrow, he would tell Michelle how Lucas had ripped up the storm.

But Ike never slapped his shoulder. Lucas sat up. He looked down the beach. Only his surfboard, alone on the sand, reflected the moon from its dinged up deck. He looked in the other direction. Ignoring their rods, staring and pointing at the ocean, the fishermen stood at the pier's railing.

Beneath the rain and the moon, the ocean surged and chopped. Lucas jumped up. "Ike!" he tried shouting above the roar of the surf. Something was bobbing out there. There was a shape in the water, but Lucas couldn't figure out what it was. He yelled again, "Ike!" Only the crashing waves answered.

The Last Thing They Ever Do

"Byron, are you smoking too?" Sarah asked.

"Yeah," Byron answered. He nodded even though she couldn't see him, and he moved the phone a bit so he could flick his cigarette in the ashtray.

"That's nice," she said. For a moment, she sounded like herself again. "Maybe I can just close my eyes and pretend like we're smoking together here."

Byron smiled sadly. He set his cigarettes and his lighter beside himself on the bed, and he leaned back to rest his head against the wall.

Sarah started talking again, "Do you remember when you used to call me every night so we could watch TV together?"

Byron smiled. His throat was dry. His mouth was hollow, but he managed to say, "Yeah."

"Well, this is just like that," she said.

"Yeah," he laughed sadly, "Just like that."

Sarah whispered, "I'm glad you're my friend." He could picture her puffy eyes and her stained cheeks lifting into a timid smile. He didn't answer her.

Sitting there, listening to one another inhale and exhale smoke, they were silent for a little while.

Sarah said, "Byron, what do you think it feels like to die?"

A weird mix of sadness and anger contorted Byron's face. He shook his head and said, "I don't know."

"Do you think it feels better than being alive?"

His bed creaked as he sat up on it. He pulled his hands down his cheeks, but he left his fingertips on his chin. "Yeah, it probably does."

"I think so too."

From the background, a woman's muffled voice yelled Sarah's name. "My mom's home. I'm not supposed to be on the phone," she sniffled.

"Are you gonna tell her?" he asked.

"Hell no," she almost laughed. "The common bastard will deny it anyway." Then, Sarah whispered his name again, and her voice got even softer, "You're my best friend."

Byron didn't answer.

Getting closer, the woman yelled again. He pictured Sarah cup her hand around her mouth. "I love you," she whispered.

"I love you too," Byron said. The other end of the phone clicked. The line went dead. Byron hung up.

Sitting still on his bed, he lit another cigarette. His room was the bowl of an ashtray. The smoke lay thick and heavy with nowhere to escape. It swirled and congealed in a heavy cloud near the ceiling. Byron stood up and stepped over the jeans and black tee shirts on his floor to open the window next to the messy dresser across from his bed. He took a deep breath of the humid air bursting in on him. Even in the night, the heat was almost unbearable, but it was preferable to the choking smoke.

The air conditioner hanging on the window next to the open one rumbled sharply beneath the light shining on it. Liquid ran down its side and dripped into a muddy puddle beneath it. The air conditioner smelled of mildew. It blew the stench into his house, and Byron hated it. He hated the way his house and his clothes and his hair stank from that machine that was supposed to make him pleasant.

He stood, leaning against the window frame, staring at the black woods beyond the shadows of pick-ups jacked up in the backyard. Sarah's house was on the other side of all that. He stretched his spine. The vertebrae cracked, and he loosely twisted his stiff neck. In the driveway to the left, the sharp outline of the rig of his dad's truck was waiting for the next job. The dark shapes of its stacks were the horns of a great beast. Its gaping grill formed the long teeth of a wired mouth. Byron pursed his lips and shook his head. "Get back on the road, old man," he whispered. He angrily flicked his cigarette into the darkness. It spun a scattering of sparks, and it dove into the ground to burn away on the grass.

Byron turned around. He ran his hands through his hair. Grabbing hold of the long, black strands, he pulled at his scalp. He wanted to scream something, but the rumble of the air conditioner and the distant crickets wouldn't be enough to bury his voice, and he knew that if he shouted anything, his dad would come in with a belt whipping through the sticky air.

A large, oval mirror was set on top of his battered dresser. In its fingerprinted glass, Byron's reflection was a little distorted, even longer and sharper than he actually was. His bare chest and arms were lankier than his sinewy body should have been. His pointed features seemed to stick out even more than usual from his dark, sunken eyes, but it was still him, with his scarred body and his long hair.

Running his hands down his legs, he leaned toward his reflection. Blowing the hair off his forehead, he set his hands on the edge of the dresser. He stared into his black eyes. "What am I supposed to do, huh?" he whispered.

"Why you tell me about that?" He slammed his hand against the hard wood of his dresser.

With a thud, it rocked back into the wall. Byron glanced over his shoulder to wait with tense breath to see whether or not his dad would come thundering into his room, but his door stayed closed. He exhaled and turned back to his eyes. As he started speaking again, he lost himself in their darkness. He spat at the mirror as if it were someone else, "How you think you can do that? What's your problem, man?" He stepped back and straightened up. The long muscles beneath the scars on his chest flexed and relaxed, "I'll kill you, man. You know that? I'll fuckin' kill you." His eyes grew wide. His head went numb, "If I ever find you, I'm gonna slit your goddamn throat." Crossing his arms and leaning toward the mirror, he ended by launching a wad of phlegm onto his reflection. The white mucus stuck then streaked down the glass. Byron turned around.

His room stank of stale sweat and smoke and fetid air. The air was too hot, too humid. The air conditioner was too loud and too monotonous. The night was too long. Byron walked over to a little, black boombox on the floor next to his bed. Cracking his knees, he crouched down to dig through a pile of tapes next to it. Picking each one up and flinging it aside with a plastic crash, scattering them across the carpet, he finally found the one he wanted to listen to. He stuck it in the boombox, pressed rewind, listened to it whir and stick, and then he stepped away and let it play.

The droning guitar filled his bedroom's sticky heat. Byron lit another cigarette that he didn't want. A deep voice swirled around him.

Walking tiny circles around his room, running his hands through his hair, Byron closed his eyes. Above the music's chant, the air conditioner still rattled his window. Byron's eyes snapped open. An old baseball trophy was on his dresser, a little figurine in a cap with a bat above his shoulder: Little League 1986. He hadn't won it for doing anything special, just for playing, and its dull color and diminutive size proved that. He snatched it off the dresser. He curled his arm back and flung the trophy out the window at the metal box. Weighted by its base, the trophy spun awkwardly through the air. A loud clank sounded as it struck the air conditioner. Leaving a dent, the batter's head snapped off, and the trophy thudded into the muddy earth. The rumble skipped a beat, knocked a bit, then grumbled even deeper than it had before.

Byron stood still, staring blankly and panting a little from the outburst. With a click and a whoosh and a slam as it hit the wall, his door flew open. Startled, he spun around.

His dad stepped into the room. "What the hell was that noise?"

Byron stayed still.

Beneath his small forehead, his dad's thick eyebrows were bunched up. His huge shoulders were hunched over his beer fed frame. His legs were sticks poking out of his shorts. As he swayed forward a little bit from the liquor, his legs looked like they might snap beneath the body they were supporting. "I asked you a question."

"Somethin' fell outside," Byron answered.

His dad's bloodshot eyes shot toward the window. He knit his eyebrows closer together. He looked back at Byron. He darted his fat tongue out to lick his penciled lips. "Whad you break, boy?"

"Nothin'. I told you it was outside."

His dad stepped forward and searched the room for signs of violence. He stared at the streaked mirror. Curling his lips, he said, "Don't lie to me, boy. I tell your P.O., and you ain't gonna have to worry 'bout this house arrest. You be locked up again."

"It was nothin'. Somethin' fell outside."

His dad wobbled there for a little while. He narrowed his eyes. He cocked his head to the side. "Turn that damn noise down," he said. "People are tryin' to sleep."

Byron nodded.

His dad turned around and slammed the door behind himself.

Byron turned the radio down. The air conditioner's racket drowned it out almost completely. Pulling at his hair and staring at the floor, Byron walked back to the mirror.

His face was pale. His heart was thumping. His breath was shaking. His palms were sweating like he was sick. Rubbing his greasy hands together, he stared in the mirror at the scars across his chest.

He traced his fingertips down their thick lines. Then, he frowned and moved one step closer to the dresser.

Opening the top drawer and pushing his underwear aside, he pulled out a piece of black metal about the length of his hand.

The metal was warm and sticky, thick and moist with either the air's or his hand's condensation. Byron pushed up on a little, silver button near the top. With a snap, a metal blade flew out the side to stick and lock when it came straight with the handle.

Lightly holding the switchblade in his right hand, Byron rubbed his thumb across the blade. The grooves in his skin caught on the sharpened metal. He blew his hair off his forehead. Cocking his head to the side, he tightened his fingers around the grip. He curled his arm to bring the blade up to touch the point against his shoulder.

He turned back to the mirror and stared at himself for a moment. The streak of mucus down his reflection looked like a tear, and he scowled. He looked back at his arm, inhaled deeply, held his breath, grit his teeth, and popped the point into his skin.

He had to close his eyes. A tiny rip followed the knife point. Easily cutting through his flesh, the metal slid smoothly down his arm. Byron winced. His eyes teared. A small whine escaped his lips. When he glanced at the mirror, a ridge of flesh around his newly made wound puffed up pink. A trickle of deep red splotches dotted the two inch long, vertical incision.

But Byron didn't look for long. He moved the knife's point. He twisted the angle of his hand. Closing his eyes and holding his breath again, he pushed the knife into his skin just a little bit to the side of the first slice that was piling blood in its groove. He grunted as he pulled the blade horizontally through his arm. Its point stuck in the first incision, and he cried out softly. "Bleed," he whispered, flexing his forearm to rip the metal through the drips of blood to continue slicing his shoulder. Byron pulled the blade out of himself. With his head alive from the pain, he opened his eyes.

The little dots of blood from the first slice had pooled and overflowed. A lake of sticky red was running down his bicep. The second slice was still fresh and pink and beginning to drip just a little bit. Byron twisted his torso to get a better look at his work. He could almost see what he had carved. Then, the horizontal incision filled and spilled another ocean.

The blood ran down his forearm and onto his hand. It dripped through the air and spilled to stain the carpet. Byron quickly dropped the knife back in the drawer. He pulled out a pair of underwear. He rubbed the cotton up his arm. Red streaks smeared across his skin, but for a moment, when he slapped the sopping fabric around his incisions, he saw the reflection of the inverted cross that he had carved into himself. But the wound quickly filled and overflowed again.

The first pair of underpants became saturated, and Byron dropped them. He grabbed another pair, but the blood flowed faster than he could clean, and he had to toss the soaked cotton aside and grab another pair. His face paled. He picked a dirty sock up off the ground. He used his hand and his teeth to tie it tight around his shoulder to try and stem the flow.

When the blood finally stopped running, Byron calmly used his last pair of underpants to wipe up what was left. His head felt light. His shoulder throbbed. The stiff sock scratched his skin. His arm felt sticky. The deep fluid had stained his flesh. Stepping backwards, he landed on his bed.

Lighting another cigarette, he leaned back and exhaled vigorously. He strained to hear the music hidden beneath the air conditioner's noise. He thought about calling Sarah back, but he knew that if her mom hadn't passed out yet, then all he'd do was get her in trouble. "If she can talk, she'll call me," he whispered.

He lay still for a little while, just smoking and staring at the ceiling and feeling his mind empty out. Glancing toward the dresser, he frowned at the missing trophy. His gaze grew bleary and indistinct when he stared at the bloodstain on his carpet and the soaked underpants scattered across his floor. He twisted his neck to check the sock. Smeared red, his arm was trembling. No more blood was flowing down his limb, but the sock was beginning to get a little soggy. He thought that maybe he should go to the bathroom to try washing himself off and finding a real dressing for his wound.

He left the stereo on. Quietly opening and closing his door, he stepped into the hallway. In the long, narrow corridor, the air conditioner was only a distant knocking.

Byron glanced to his right. A TV's blue tint lit the darkness at that end. The murmur of speakered voices added a touch of life to the otherwise dismal house. He heard the heavy creak of his dad's chair and the distant tinkle of ice cubes knocking against glass. Byron turned in the other direction to head toward the bathroom.

"Byron?" a timid voice asked. He turned back around.

His little brother was standing there, wearing the pajamas that he always seemed to wear. His hair was a mess from tossing around in his sleep. Byron didn't say anything. The little boy shuffled a little bit closer. "Byron, are you okay?"

The child's eyes were wide and terrified. Dropping down almost to his level, Byron leaned closer to his brother. The older brother blew his hair off his forehead. He whispered, "Go back to bed, Michael. You shouldn't be up right now."

"I heard a noise earlier. It woke me up."

"Everything's okay," Byron whispered. "Go back to bed before dad sees you're still up."

The little boy pulled nervously at his ear. "I had a bad dream."

Byron nodded. He straightened back up. "Just go back to bed."

Michael's mouth dropped open. Terrified, he whispered, "What happened to your arm?"

Byron shrugged, "Don't worry about it." He turned around to try and make it to the bathroom before his dad heard them whispering.

But before he had even taken a step, he heard the heavy swing of his dad's chair and the thud of the man's feet. Byron dropped his head. Then, the shout came, "Michael! Get your ass back in that room, boy! What the hell you still doin' up?"

The pitter-patter of Michael running along the carpet led to the click and slam of the little boy's bedroom door. Byron turned around just in time to see his brother reaching up to fumblingly grab the handle and pull it back toward his scared face.

His dad flicked the hall light on. Blinded, Byron squinted at its yellow brilliance. "I told you people were tryin' to sleep, boy," his dad slurred and stumbled forward, bracing himself against the hallway.

Careful to keep his shoulder out of the old man's sight, Byron tried heading off to the bathroom. "Goddamnit! Look at me when I'm..." His dad stopped talking as Byron turned back to face him. The man's gaze steamed. His eyebrows fumed. "What the hell you do to yourself?"

Byron glanced at his shoulder. Turning back to his dad, he slowly answered, "I caught my arm on a nail."

His dad thudded toward him. At sixteen, Byron was about an inch taller than him, but the man's shoulders seemed almost as broad as the hall. His chest was as solid as the grill of his truck. Byron wondered for a moment if his own long build would ever puff out like his father's. A spasm of disgust passed over his face.

"That's bull shit, boy." He reached out and yanked on Byron's arm. Pain shot from Byron's shoulder to his brain. He winced, but his dad didn't notice. He swayed a little bit, taking in the dark shadow of stained skin, staring at the sock growing dark and moist. Flinging his son's arm away from himself, he shouted, "Jesus Christ! What the hell is wrong with you?"

Byron gently rubbed his throbbing shoulder. He shrugged and turned around.

"Where you think you're goin'?"

"To clean myself up."

"It don't matter how clean you get yourself. You be

back in that detention center 'fore you can spit."

Hiding his eyes behind his hair, Byron glared over his shoulder, but his dad had already turned to head back to the TV's glow.

Shaking his head, Byron walked to the bathroom. Beneath the quivering light, the walls' peeling paint and the sink's dirty basin seemed like post-apocalyptic remnants of some ancient, once habitable society. The exposed pipes knocked as Byron turned the grimy faucet.

He ran the water into his cupped hands, leaned down, and splashed it across his face. A few strands of hair stuck to his forehead. The drips glistened on his pale skin. His lips quivered in time to the seemingly dying light. The sock around his shoulder was scratching him less and less as it grew damper.

Byron splashed some more water onto his forearm. As he massaged it across his skin, it dripped back into the sink, pink. He turned off the faucet. Feeling a little lightheaded, he leaned against the wall opposite the sink and the mirror.

Dotted by months of stray spray, the mirror reflected a pointillist portrait of him. Exhaling, Byron glanced up and blew the hair off his eyes. The movement of air agitated the house's stench. Byron clenched his fist. In a tight, barely forceful arc, he swung it back into the wall. "Oh God, I hate this shit," he whispered.

Leaning over to his left, he turned the faucet on in the bathtub. A thick downpour of water splashed against the porcelain. Byron slipped out of his tight jeans. He leaned over to check the tub's temperature. Drawing the stained shower curtain, he flipped the little switch between the knobs on the faucet. Sputtering, the shower started up. Byron stepped out of his underwear, kicked it to the side, and stepped into the shower.

The tub's floor was slick and slimy. The water didn't

drain quite right. It pooled in an almost gray puddle streaked with strands of long hair. Curling his lips back and closing his eyes, Byron touched his toes against the puddle so that he could step beneath the spray. Slick and hot, the water drenched his makeshift bandage. It pounded the smeared blood off Byron's arm to leave a light pool of pink that ran to the drain and swirled in with the grayness and the hair. In the middle of the shower's torrent, running his hands through his hair, slicking its strands onto his back and neck, without moving his lips, Byron whispered, so softly that even if anybody had been there they wouldn't have heard, "Why can't it just end?"

There was a crash and a thud and a curse. Byron's eyes popped open. He jumped just a little bit. The soap slipped out of his hands, but before he could lean down to pick it up, the rattling rings on the shower curtain slid across the rusted rod. With a whoosh, the curtain billowed back. Byron caught a glimpse of his father before a whir sliced through the air to end in a wet smack that stung his ribs.

Byron whimpered slightly. He slipped and stumbled backward into the tiles, but before he fell, the belt flew through the air again to lash his shoulder and leave a long, red welt. "What is your problem, boy!" his dad shouted, and the belt struck him again.

Byron banged his elbow against the tub. He breathed a pathetic sound. His feet splashed in the puddle as he tried regaining his breath and sense. Scurrying in every direction, he scrambled into the tub's corner, balling his legs up to his chest, instinctively trying to protect himself as his stunned mind tried to understand what was going on.

Trying to get closer to his son, his dad put one foot in the tub. The steaming water drenched his shorts and his thin, hairy legs. The belt came at Byron again. He brought his hands up to protect his face. The leather smacked his palms. It whirred around his head to slap his ear. For a moment, Byron couldn't hear anything on his right side, but his left ear still heard what his dad was saying. Each word was punctuated by the motion of the belt. Each slap of the belt ended in Byron's gasps. "What the hell is wrong with you, boy? Why's there blood all over your goddamn room?" Byron tried dodging and blocking the belt. His mind was coming back to him. As he grew used to them, the stings from the whips weren't hurting quite so bad. He narrowed his eyes. He clenched his teeth. He stopped recoiling into the corner. He just listened to the belt smack his skin.

"And tell your little whore people are tryin' to sleep here!" With his features on fire, Byron turned his head up to stare blankly at his old man. His dad brought the belt back again. It whirred through the air above his head, but when his arm came straight, the belt stopped for a moment. It wrapped and slapped around the curtain rod. His dad looked up, grunted, and pulled. The rod came loose from the wall. Tangling around the man's pudgy hands, the curtain crashed into the tub.

With both hands in front of himself, Byron jumped up. He used the extra force from his spring to ram his palms into his dad's chest. Stumbling backward, his dad knocked his heel against the tub. Beneath the falling, billowing shower curtain, the top-heavy man crashed to the floor. He braced himself with his arms and drunkenly mumbled something. Then, his hands twisted out from underneath him. His head slammed into the tiles.

Byron slipped a little, but he quickly steadied himself. The water was pounding across his naked frame. His pulse was racing, and his arm was trembling. He looked down at his dad. The man's eyes were closed. He was moving his jaw in heavy, drunken breaths. He was slowly rolling his head as if his numbed mind were having a bad dream and it was trying to figure out what was happening. But Byron didn't wait. He leaped out of the tub and skidded across the tiles to the door.

Michael was standing still in the hallway, still in his pajamas, still with his hair a mess. His lips were trembling. His eyes were puffy, and he was sniffling. He blubbered something when his brother came out of the bathroom, but Byron wasn't listening. "Get outta here," he whispered, stumbling past him.

The door to his bedroom was open. Off the hook and beeping, the phone was lying on his bed. The stereo was still droning beneath the air conditioner's rattle. The voice was breathing, palpitating. And then with a crunch, the music rushed in again.

Still naked, staring at the bloody underwear, Byron walked a few small circles. His entire body was shaking. His breath was jagged. He ran his hand through his sopping hair. "Sarah," he whispered, and he quickly reached down to wriggle his wet legs into a skin-tight pair of faded, ripped up jeans. The denim clung to the moisture. It scratched his skin.

Hurriedly sitting down on the floor, he slipped on a pair of black high tops. Standing back up, he squashed his soaking feet into the soles. He grabbed a black tee shirt and ran over to the dresser.

From the mirror, he caught a glimpse of his reflection. His face was as white as a sun-bleached skull. Water drained like a deluge from his long hair. The sock around his arm was soaked a deep red color. Raised welts were slashed across his wet, dripping neck, arms, shoulders, and chest. One stripe even skidded around the right side of his face. Byron twisted his lips. Screaming, he reached out, grabbed the mirror, and toppled it onto the floor where the glass crashed and splintered into myriad little slivers.

He slipped the shirt over his scarred torso. The sleeve puffed out around the sock on his shoulder. Reaching into the top drawer, he grabbed the switchblade, closed and locked it, and fumblingly shoved it into his back pocket.

He slipped his hands through his hair to slick it back out of his eyes, and he walked over to the window. The air conditioner stank and grumbled at him. Byron flung the glass up hard enough to make it rattle in its frame. He threw one leg over the sill. The distant sound of his father grumbling reached his ear. Byron ducked out into the night.

He landed in mud, on the base of the trophy. He stumbled a little bit, and his ankle twisted. A few of the mildewed drops from the air conditioner landed on him, but soon he was running, limping as if he had a clubfoot, past the jacked-up pick-up trucks. His dad's rig glared at his back, but it couldn't catch him now. Byron breathed heavily and pumped his arms as he headed toward the woods. Sarah lived on the other side.

A First Attempt at Flying

On the outskirts of the subdivision, beyond the skeletal construction sites, in the middle of a wasteland of rutted dirt, was Skill Hill. It was part of a ditch, a chasm that cut a circle at least 20 feet deep out of the earth. It plummeted down from the wasteland, bottomed out in a murky stream dotted with shrubs well fed by the sewage, and rose again into an island cut off from the rest of the land by the ditch itself.

But Skill Hill was only a piece of that ditch. It was a concrete wall that kept the earth from collapsing beneath gravity. It was a smooth rectangle of white cement slapped onto the rain-beaten terrain. It was a 20 foot descent, 30 feet wide, that was perfect for a bicycle.

Only the neighborhood's bravest kids ventured there to force their bicycles' thin wheels down the wall. With the wind rushing on their teeth, they would pedal as hard as they could. Furiously increasing down the cement, their speeds would top out just as their bikes reached the dark drainage's closest laps. It was there, right at the water's edge, with a sudden pull of the handlebars, that the bikes were supposed to screech their terror, their pleasure, whatever it was that happened at the bottom of Skill Hill, and if the kids had done what they needed to do, if they could look back over their shoulders and see that a beautiful, black skid marked the cement so close to the water that tiny waves would wash across it, then they had conquered the hill. Grinning triumphantly, they could sit beside the water and stare at the little island that was cut off from the rest of the earth.

Otherwise, if there were any hesitation, if even for a moment the idea of skidding at that speed was too frightening, the bike would stay silent. With a wide arcing swoop, the downward momentum would carry the kids back to where they had come from. Without them having to pump their pedals even once, Skill Hill would spew them from its depths.

Earlier that day, the brothers had planned to ride around on the streets near their home, but the summer's heat and humidity had driven everybody to the pools, leaving the subdivision's streets empty. The two elder boys, leading the way, riding without using their hands, were talking to each other. Carey was staring at a bird when he heard them mention Skill Hill.

Now, as the three of them swung their freewheeling pedals and swerved their front tires, the skids stole their gazes. From the top of the hill to the bottom, the dark marks increased from the kids who had ventured deeper and deeper into the depths. Some of the skids were only timidly short, smeared stains. Others were the picture-perfect remnant of a kid who had attempted the hill.

Two of the marks were made by the two oldest brothers. Carey hadn't yet watched his front tire dip off of the earth.

Burning between cotton-white puffs of clouds, the sun scorched their three throats parched even in the moist summer. The light and the heat separated the water from the sewage. It pulled the liquid out from between the shrubs – the only life in that desolation outside the subdivision – and left the drops evaporated in the air. The humidity stuck to the brothers' skin, and even though it condensed in their lungs, it didn't water the earth. The dust, crossed and marked by kids who had pedaled through the fall's mud, was reddish brown and motionless around the three brothers who were all wearing tee shirts and shorts and all staring at the descent.

Being the oldest, Gabe was the first to break the silence. He kicked the kickstand on his blue BMX Racer. The bike tilted to its side, and he set his feet on the ground. "We shouldn't even be here," he panted into the humidity.

Seth was pedaling backwards and forwards as his red Diamondback wobbled beneath his attempts to keep it balanced. At Gabe's words, he thrust his own kickstand into the earth. He glared at the brother who was barely one year older than him. "Well, Carey said he wanted to try it." He glanced back over his shoulder. "Didn't you, Carey?"

Startled, Carey glanced up from the ditch. Both of his brothers were staring at him. The little boy couldn't do anything more than blink at the identical faces wearing different expressions on their different colorings. When his mouth moved and no sound came out, he swallowed to try to stick some saliva together. Staring at Seth, he stuttered, "Yeah... Yeah, I did." Then, he glanced at Gabe and went back to looking down the ditch.

Sighing, Gabe said, "Well, if I let you guys come all the way out here, then I guess I have to let Carey try it."

"Oh come on, Gabe" Seth whined, "Nobody put you in charge. You didn't 'let' us come here."

"Yeah, I know, but you know Mom and Dad would flip if they knew you came out here with him, and if I'm here too..." he ended by shaking his head.

"It's all right, Gabe," Carey whispered, "I wanted to

come."

Leaning over his handlebars, Gabe looked past Seth at Carey. Carey was too young to break the same sweat that the heat and exertion brought out on his older brothers. He was simply leaning forward, resting his chin on the checkered pad softening the crossbar between the handles.

"Yeah, this is definitely a mistake," Gabe said, almost to himself.

But Seth heard him, and he spat, "Jesus, Gabe. It's not like we didn't do it."

"Yeah, but I wasn't not allowed, and you just did it anyway."

Shaking his head, Seth laughed, "So you can go down Skill Hill just cuz Mom and Dad never said you weren't allowed?"

With his toe, Gabe picked at a pebble wedged into the dirt. The tiny rock popped out of the ground. He frowned and said, "Yeah, but as soon as I told them about it, none of us were allowed."

"And so Gabe's allowed to do things that we're not?" Seth mocked.

Gabe ground his teeth. Kicking the pebble into the ditch, he reminded his brother, "You did it too."

"Yeah, but I got grounded as soon as Mom and Dad found out where I'd been."

"Well, you shouldn't have told them."

"Did you want me to lie when I came home after dark?"

"So, what, you wanna get Carey in trouble too?"

"Nobody's getting in trouble, Gabe. If he wants to try it, then you gotta watch him. We gotta be here to prove our little brother went down Skill Hill. At least, I know I wanna be here. Right, Carey?"

Picking his chin up from his crossbar, Carey answered,

"Sure," but he added, "Don't worry, Gabe, I can do it."

"Whether you can do it or not doesn't matter. Mom and Dad say we're not even allowed to be here. That means that if anything happens, even if we're just not home on time, then we're all gonna get in trouble. That means you too, Seth."

Seth looked down the hill. "Nothing's gonna happen," he said.

"Look. If anything happens – I mean *any*thing, I'd be responsible…"

"What the hell could possibly happen?"

Gabe didn't respond.

"Fine," Seth hissed, "But if Carey wants to try it, then who are you to say he can't?"

"Who am I? I'm his oldest brother."

"Yeah, well I'm his brother too, but I know that he should be able to do what he wants."

Just like when he had puffed and pedaled so hard to catch up to his brothers riding through the neighborhood, to tell them that he wanted to go to Skill Hill *today*, Carey quietly entered the conversation, "I don't see what the big deal is, Gabe."

Both of his brothers stared at him. Gabe tilted his head, creased his eyes, and pursed his lips. Seth flashed a grin that neither of his brothers ever made.

"Carey, look down that hill," Gabe said quietly.

The cement dropped into the ditch. The dark water sat still between the shrubs. Gabe spoke again, "Do you know what's in that water?"

Carey shook his head.

"You see all the spots, they look kinda like rain drops even though there's no rain?"

Carey nodded.

"Every single one of those little spots is a mosquito.

They lay their eggs in the water, and they live down there. Nobody goes down Skill Hill without getting bit. As soon as your bike stops, when you skid, it's like they knew you were coming. They swarm all over you." Carey bit his lip. His brother kept talking, "Plus, there's snakes down there, Carey – water moccasins. They live in the bushes, and they swim underwater. So if you're down there, you can't even see them coming. That's why Mom and Dad don't want us here."

Carey's eyes grew wide. He wasn't scared of the mosquitoes. They lived everywhere, but he thought he saw a snake slither through the brush and drop into the water. Its scales reflected the sun. Then, it was gone. Carey scanned the stream. He was almost certain that he could see the snake beneath the water.

Carey choked and coughed. The sun beat down on his neck. He finally started sweating a bit on the back of his neck. He wiped it off, but he couldn't look away from the cottonmouth at the bottom of Skill Hill.

"Is that what you're afraid of, Gabe?" Seth laughed, "Cuz Carey could be bit by a mosquito anywhere. Just cuz they're born down there doesn't mean…"

"It's not the mosquitoes, Seth. The only big deal about them is that if he comes home all bit up, and we're not, Mom and Dad are gonna wonder how that happened…"

"So you're afraid of the snakes?"

Gabe didn't answer.

"Carey," Seth smiled, "Snakes aren't a big deal."

"What do you know about snakes?"

"I know a lot about 'em, Gabe."

Gabe shrugged, but Seth didn't notice. He kept talking to Carey, "Look, Carey, you can catch any snake down there."

"What are you talking about, Seth?"

Standing up on his pedals, Seth blocked the sun and shouted, "I catch 'em all the time, Gabe!"

Gabe twisted his features. He didn't believe Seth, but Seth didn't pay any attention to him. Still standing on his pedals, still casting a shadow over Carey, he told him, "The snakes swim underwater, Carey, but as long as you stay at the edge, you can see 'em comin'. Then, when they crawl up from the sewer, you gotta sneak up behind 'em, and if you grab 'em right behind the head, they can't bite you. Once you got 'em, you can do anything you want with 'em," and Seth reached down to mimic the action of catching the snake.

Smiling and still holding the imaginary snake in his hand, he plopped back into his seat. The sun reappeared, and Carey squinted. He was speechless. When he looked back into the ditch, the water moccasin he thought he had seen was nowhere near as scary as Gabe had made it sound.

"And you've done that before, huh, Seth?"

"Yeah, Gabe, I've done it."

Gabe didn't say anything.

"Gabe, if the snakes don't matter like Seth says, then why does it matter if I try Skill Hill?"

Gabe looked down the ditch. One long and dark streak near the bottom caught his gaze. A long time ago, when the seat he was sitting on hadn't been much higher than Carey's, that mark had been screamed into existence by his own BMX. Thinking, he frowned. "Carey," he said, "Do you see that one mark down there by the water?"

Carey tried looking where his brother was pointing.

"I made that mark," he said, "You know you don't have to go any closer to the water than right there. Okay?"

Carey nodded.

"Except," Seth added, "You can't even *see* my mark. The water's too high right now."

Gabe scowled at Seth. Seth smiled at Carey. Carey breathed deeply.

"Go ahead," Gabe said.

Carey swallowed hard. Exhaling slowly, he tightened his hands on the handlebars.

"You're gonna wanna back up some," Seth told him, "So you can get good speed."

Carey lifted his kickstand off the ground. He stood up on his pedals. He pressed down with his left leg. Swerving back around, his little Diamondback jumbled through the ruts.

A short distance away, he heard Gabe call, "That's good Carey!" He stopped pedaling, and he turned back to see Gabe and Seth sitting at the edge of the ditch.

The sun burned above them. Skill Hill loomed before them. Its bottom was invisible now. A trickle of sweat dripped down Carey's forehead. It stung his eyes. "Go ahead," Seth told him.

Carey pressed down on the pedals. The chain spun. It pulled the back tire along. Bobbing up and down, building his bike's speed, Carey rumbled through the rutted dirt. Both of his brothers turned to watch him.

The heat folded the earth. The humidity got thicker. Skill Hill opened up in front of Carey. Coming closer to his brothers, he swallowed and held his breath. Soon, he was alongside them. Then, his front tire dipped off the ground.

Still pedaling as hard as he could, he was flying down the cement. The glittering surface slipped away. A whooshing noise rushed across his ears. He could see the pinpricked bodies of the mosquitoes. They were raindrops on the black stream. Carey sped over the skid marks. The air smelled dead. The world was zooming past quicker than Carey could have imagined. The smell got stronger. He reached Gabe's mark, but he kept going, trying to find

Seth's invisible mark.

At the water's edge, he inhaled the ditch's decay. He stopped pedaling. Spinning faster than it should, his front tire passed off the concrete onto a patch of asphalt that was permanently stained by the sewage. Carey strained to pull the handlebars. With a cry, a spray of murky water skidded out from beneath his tires to drench his Diamondback's blue frame. Below the earth, as a sheen of mud slipped between his wheels and the ground, Carey saw the world tilt.

For a moment, he really was flying. In that second, he thought that maybe he had gone as far as Seth had, but then, his wings melted. With a small splash, he fell into the water.

He kept his eyes closed. His palms, his elbows, his knees were burning from their slide across the concrete that wasn't quite so smooth when you got so close to it. The rocks in it had sliced off pieces of his flesh, and each one released its own piece into the drainage flowing overtop of it. This far into the ditch, the smell was so strong. Carey tried focusing on it so that his body wouldn't hurt so bad.

Then, a buzz beside his ear and a prick in the back of his neck made him start up. He inhaled a short breath of sewage. Not too far away from him, he couldn't see the bottom of the stream. Something darted beneath the surface, and Carey scrambled back onto the concrete.

Still spinning its wheels, his bike was on its side, but a brand new mark was on the cement. Small waves licked the twisted handlebars. Breathing deeply, Carey scooted beside his bike. The sudden motion hurt his hands. They bled a trail from where he had been to where he was now.

The smell swirled through the air that was too humid to evaporate the water sticking to Carey's arms and face and clothes. He looked at his hands and elbows and knees.

Blood was dripping from the maroon scrapes and the deep gashes that had infected him. Mosquitoes landed on him, taking a piece of him away with every buzz of their wings. Carey felt his cool blood wash across the warm sludge caked to his knees. He was about to cry.

Then, a scream echoed down through Skill Hill. With sweat stuck to his forehead, Carey turned to the sound. The sun was behind his brothers. In order to see them, he had to shade his eyes.

Both of his brothers were shadows now. They looked exactly the same. Only their mannerisms revealed their names. Raised high in the air, both of Seth's fists were punching holes in the sky. With a grin on his mud-splattered face, Carey lifted his arms to mirror his action. Gabe hung his head over his arms folded across his handlebars, and he shouted, "Come back, Carey!"

Suddenly, amid a clatter of metal on metal on earth, Gabe and Seth dropped their bikes and leaped into the ditch to run down the cement wall. Gabe was yelling something about getting out of there, but the words didn't make any sense. And Carey couldn't understand why Seth was staring at something to his left.

Slowly dropping his arms, Carey turned to see what Seth was running at.

The water moccasin must have been woken up by the screaming bike splashing into the ditch. Now, its tongue was flickering back and forth as it slithered into the light to sun its whip-like body on the concrete. Carey stopped breathing. He wanted to escape, but he couldn't move.

The sun baked everything it came into contact with. Skill Hill's dead smell permeated the air. Drops of water pooled around Carey. Mosquitoes were buzzing everywhere. Drops of blood dripped onto the concrete. Hissing at Carey, the snake revealed the cotton-white mouth behind its fangs. Seth shouted to his paralyzed, baby brother, "Get up and catch it, Carey! Catch the snake!"

Somewhere I've Never Been

This story happened before I was born. And it happened in places I've never been to. But something that is so intricately interwoven into the fabric of who you are paralyzes your mind and forces you to look at it until it gains a vibrancy brighter than the tapestry of your own memories.

It started in the summer of 1967, the summer of love. It was before the fall of the seventies, before the winter of the eighties, and long before the strange world we live in today.

Sometimes I think the Cold War did end in a hot one, at least in our minds, and we've been immobilized by some sort of psychic nuclear freeze ever since. But spring has to come again. So I'll try sowing the seeds left over from our last summer, and I'll pray that the world is finally fertile enough to take them again.

Evie lived in an apartment in the Haight District. From behind her blinds, she looked out on a world colored by flowers and their children.

She told me that when the first letter came, she didn't recognize the handwriting. The military postmark was strange, and the last name didn't register with her. When she opened it, she scrunched up her eyes, leaned deeper into her beanbag chair, and flipped the pages over to check the signature.

Her heart thumped once, twice, and then, for all she knew, it stopped. That's what she says. She wasn't paying attention to it anymore. Staring at the name, she sat completely still. Her fingers loosened on the pages. The papers would have fallen to the floor if she hadn't tightened her grasp to turn the letter back over, to read it slowly, taking her time with every word.

By the end, she had stopped breathing. She reread the letter a few times. Then, she dropped the letter into her lap, and she sat completely still, staring out the sunny window in front of her.

The noise of cars and people in the street rose up to her. She folded the letter back up, put it in the envelope, walked into her bedroom, put the letter in her desk drawer, lay down on her bed, and closed her eyes.

The letter stayed in her drawer for weeks. But she thought about it. She thought about the boy she had known for a few weeks who was now in Vietnam. He had been so nice.

One night, she had a dream about him. In her dream, she was looking for him everywhere, on the streets of San Francisco, on her college campus, in the halls of her old high school, on the playgrounds she had played at as a child. In her dream, she found him burning in a village she had seen on TV.

Her eyes snapped open to her dark room. Even though the dream was over, she could still feel the terror of its presence. Her heart was racing. Something was chasing her. She tried balling herself into the corner of her bed, but even in the night, she could still hear the sounds of San Francisco, the town across the Bay from that young boy's home.

For the first time in months, she could see his smiling

face clearly in her mind.

She sat up in bed. Her throat was blocked, and her head was numb. She walked over to her desk, switched on a lamp, and pulled a pen and a piece of paper out of her drawer. She set the tip of the pen on the page, and she started to write. By the time she was done saying what she wanted to say, she was crying.

Andy found a tree that he could sit beneath. It was far enough away from everything that he couldn't hear the shouts and the curses, but it wasn't so far away that he was in any real danger.

The jungle rose up all around him. The sun was merciless, and the heat and humidity were unbearable, but he had endured it all this long, and he had to believe that he could endure until it was over.

Making himself more comfortable, he shifted around on the roots. He wiped the sweat from his forehead, cleaned his hands on his fatigues, and ripped the envelope open.

Careful not to drip any sweat on it, careful not to smear any grime across it, he pulled the letter from the envelope and unfolded it. He scooted around a little bit more, and then he looked down at the pages. He didn't look up until he was done. That's what he always says.

When he was done, he held the letter in his hands for a long time. His eyes teared up. His lips were trembling. There was a lump in his throat, but he felt electrified from the embodied presence that the pages sent through his fingers. He sniffled and wiped his nose and made sure to dry his hands before touching the letter again.

The sun shined through the trees. The air breathed with moisture. Bugs and snakes were slithering in the jungle behind him, but they weren't touching him. Somebody out there wanted to kill him, but all he could think about were the San Francisco Bay's cool breezes and the soft sound of Evie's voice. He realized that despite all his fears, despite everything he had seen and done, he was still human, and he would still be human when he stepped off a plane and back onto U.S. soil.

"You don't know me, man!" Andy shouted, and he stood up from the table. The scent of smoke and food filled every breath, and Andy took a deep one.

Everybody at the table was staring at him, Evie and Isaac and Renee and Frank. Their superior looks and their frightened glances greeted his reaction. He was trembling from the inside out. He leaned forward, set his knuckles on the table, and went on, calmer than he had been before. "You don't know what I saw and what I did, and you'll never know how much of it I didn't want to do. Christ, you'll never even know how much of it I didn't even want to *see*. But I had to. If it had all been up to me, none of this would have happened. I would have spent my entire life right here. But it *did* happen, and I did what I had to do."

He didn't wait for the response. He looked everybody over, and he turned around and left the restaurant.

Evie can have her friends, he thought as he thrust the door open and stepped into the San Francisco night.

His breath rose into the streetlights. The air was cool. It softened his temper. His stomach twisted and turned. He thought about turning around and walking back in and asking Evie if she wanted to come with him or else ending the whole thing with an act of violence against that boy who would judge him because of something that wasn't his fault. He could do that, too. He could end it forever. He knew he could. Taking another deep breath, he smiled sadly, and he shook his head.

"That wasn't too cool," he whispered.

With his trembling hands, he shook out a cigarette and put it in his mouth. Tilting his head to the side, he lit it.

He walked a little ways away from the restaurant door, and he leaned back against a brick wall. Evie's apartment wasn't too far from there, but he wasn't sure if he could still go there or not.

"I could find a hotel," he mumbled.

He tapped his head against the wall. An over-abundance of emotions swelled inside of him.

Grinding his teeth together, he spat, "Fuck it."

With another drag off his cigarette, he looked down the street away from the restaurant. That was the direction he would start walking in when his cigarette was done.

Her voice was soft. Her tone was hesitant: "Andy?" Her shoes clicked on the sidewalk as she came closer.

He heard her, but he didn't turn around.

With a quick staccato, her steps stopped. She whispered his name again, and she touched his arm.

Slowly, he turned around. His face was angry, but his eyes were hurt.

Evie frowned. She reached her fingers up to touch his cheek, but she stopped before she got there. She dropped her hand back to her side.

Looking at the ground, she breathed heavily. "I'm so sorry, Andy. Frank was way out of line."

Andy grunted. He looked past her through the mist to where the street began rising into a hill. He narrowed his eyes.

Evie looked at him. Through the beard hiding his face, she could read everything he was feeling even though she didn't know the reasons. She looked concerned. "I know you probably don't want to, but you should come back with me."

Andy pursed his lips.

"Frank and Isaac both said they were sorry. Everybody wants you to come back inside."

"You've got to be joking," Andy mumbled.

"Andy." She slid her hand down his arm, leaving her fingers dangling out of his loose hand. "Frank didn't mean anything. We never should have started talking about politics."

Andy shook his head. "It doesn't matter."

She tried holding his hand, but he wouldn't respond.

"Do you want to go home?" she asked. "We can do that."

He looked at her.

She nodded slightly and smiled a little. "Just let me get my stuff," she said.

She turned around, but Andy suddenly grabbed her hand. Startled, she faced him.

"Evie, will you promise me something?"

She nodded.

"Promise me that you'll never judge me for anything I tell you."

Evie stared at him for a little while. Then, she whispered, "I never would."

"There were so many things that I had to do."

Evie nodded. "I know."

Andy's eyes opened wide. All of the sadness and hurt that he had been trying to hide glowed in them.

Evie whispered something, and she reached up to hug him. He hugged her back so much tighter than she held him.

"I'm gonna go get my stuff," she said.

Andy sniffled. He nodded.

When she went back inside, he leaned back into the

wall, and he lit another cigarette. He whispered, "I can't take this anymore."

Evie walked back up to him. "Ready?" she asked.

He nodded. They started walking together down the street to her apartment.

After a few steps, Andy said, "Evie, I don't know how much longer I can stay here."

She nodded. She kept walking, but she hung her head a little.

"I don't know," he went on, "Everything with you… The whole time I was over there, this was everything I dreamed about, but I don't belong in this city anymore."

"I know."

"I don't belong around your friends. They're fine, but this isn't the first time I've felt like this around them. It's just the first time I said anything."

"I know."

"I mean, I want to go to school, but I don't think I should do it here."

Evie nodded. "Then let's go somewhere else."

Andy stopped walking. "What?"

Evie stopped too. She looked at Andy. "Let's go somewhere else, I said. Unless you don't want me to come."

He didn't move. He didn't say anything. He smiled. "Of course I want you to come," he said.

Evie smiled back at him. She walked up to him. "Good," she said, "Let's talk about it tomorrow. Tonight, let's go home and go to bed."

She stood up on her tiptoes. Andy leaned forward. Beneath the streetlight shrouded in mist, they kissed.

They did talk about it the next day. They didn't leave right away, but eventually, they did. They moved to the other side of the country, and Andy went to college. He studied political science, and his professors thought that someday they might find him in academia, but Andy knew that there was nothing scientific about politics. Politics were children from the human mind, and the human mind didn't function scientifically. Andy knew that. He'd watched it. He'd lived it. After leaving school, he disappeared into regular life, into business. Evie became a teacher.

Eventually, they were married, and they had a son, their only child. They named him after his father: Andrew. That's me. We didn't live happily ever after. We didn't live together for very long at all.

I Think I'm Ready Now

The night before I graduated from college, my parents took the family out for dinner. Afterwards, my brothers and I went out for drinks. I took the two of them to Bukowski's, my favorite bar. It was one, dark, cozy room with a long bar to your left as you walked in, smoky tables to your right, a neon sign in the window, and either punk or metal or techno blaring out of the speakers depending on who the bartender was. That night, it was punk.

Gabe looked around a little before he led us over to a table. He seemed to be sniffing the air and finding a vague scent that he found mildly displeasing. "Nice place," he said, but I think he was too enthralled with the idea of me graduating to really care. Otherwise, I'm sure he would have suggested that we go somewhere else.

Seth seemed to kind of like the place though. He had a hard time keeping his eyes off of two leather clad girls at the bar, but he managed to keep an air of superiority about himself. His body language implied that although he might have been there, he was better than the place.

I sat down against the wall. Gabe was across from me. Seth faced us on a perpendicular to my right and Gabe's left.

A waitress came over to take our orders. She was blonde and cute. Seth smiled at her when she spoke. I liked it when he smiled like that. His lips curled out like the Joker's, and his eyes lit up like he was insane. It was one expression that was entirely his own. For all their similarities, Gabe never looked like that. The waitress walked away. Seth craned his neck to watch her hips sway. Gabe laughed a little about that.

We talked until the waitress came back and set our drinks down. We raised our glasses. They met above the middle of the table in a toast to me and my future, and we didn't even spill a drop of foam. We each took a swig of beer. I leaned back into the wall and wiped a little dribble off my lips.

We laughed about our family. Gabe and Seth reminisced about their graduations and what they'd done immediately after: how hard Seth had worked to make money; how nervous Gabe had been about whether or not he'd do well in med school.

Finally, Gabe said, "So tomorrow's the big day?" He was smiling. His skin was still as smooth and fair as when we were children. It hardly wrinkled at all.

I looked down at my beer, narrowed my eyes, and nodded.

"And you're gonna be coming back to New York?"

I nodded again.

Gabe stopped smiling. He took another sip, smacked his lips, and went on, more soberly than before. "I guess you're staying with Mom and Dad, but you know you're welcome to stay with Ariel and me until you find your own place."

"Thanks, but I..."

Just like when we were kids, unable to be outdone, Seth broke in, "I don't know if Mom and Dad told you, but it's fine for you to stay in the city with me for a little while too. I could even ask around the firm to see if any positions are opening up. It would be entry level, so there wouldn't be much money at first, but it would be enough to live on, and once you start learning how the market works, you could move up. You're smart. I'm sure it wouldn't be too hard for you to figure out, and then you could make bank, if you know what I mean." Seth tipped his beer towards me, and he flashed the same grin he'd grinned earlier.

I took another sip of beer, sighed, and glanced around. I didn't know how to have that conversation right then. I nodded politely and said, "Thanks guys. Really, thanks."

Gabe and Seth each smiled their older-brother-helping-out-the-baby smiles. Gabe leaned across the table, grabbed my arm, and said something about the benefit of family. We all drank from our glasses again.

My brothers both look exactly like our father. They both have long noses, thin faces, and full lips. If it weren't for their differences in coloring – Seth's dark curls and almost olive skin, Gabe's blond hair and fair features – they could be twins. Their personalities are different as well. Seth was so cool and uncaring. Gabe was so intense and powerful.

Their oppositions formed my earliest memories. In my mind, the beginning of my life had always consisted of the two of them arguing with each other about what part I should play in their games or else each of them pulling me aside separately to give me advice about what I should or shouldn't do. Then, they'd both disappeared, and I'd still had a lot of growing up to do.

With barely a year separating them, Gabe and Seth were the brothers. I was an only child whose link to them was spending my entire life being punished for whatever mistakes they had made when they were whatever age I was at. For Christ's sake, they grew up in Texas. I grew up in New Jersey. I was nine years old when we moved. Gabe and Seth were seventeen and sixteen respectively. I was starting middle school when Seth left. They didn't know me at all. I didn't even look like them. You wouldn't think we were related unless you saw a family photo. There were plenty of those being taken that week. We were more related than we had ever been.

I look like our mother. I always have. I have brown hair. My nose is squat. My face is round. As I get older and my metabolism slows down, I'm sure I'll get fat. But right now, I look okay. It took me twenty-two years to realize that. Gabe and Seth seemed to have each known it about themselves from the day they were born. At least, that's what the awkward pre-pubescent me had always thought as I grew up, aghast at the powers that were my brothers.

And because of that, they had had as much authority over my childhood as any adult. Even more because their proximity to me had instilled a certain awe that could never be replicated by any of the giants whose stomping grounds were well outside my sphere of play.

So I wanted to understand them. So I acted as them. As soon as I entered the theater when I was in high school, I was always one of them onstage because there was nothing spectacular about me.

Gabe smiled proudly, "Mom and Dad are so happy you're gonna be close to the family again. I'm happy about it."

I politely acquiesced with what had become my habitual nod.

"Yeah," Seth laughed, "It'll be nice to tour around the city with my baby brother."

My face reddened, and I shifted around uncomfortably.

Gabe cast a mistrustful glance at Seth. Seth shrugged, *What?* It was a replay of my childhood. Growing serious again, Gabe looked back at me and asked, "So what *are* you planning on doing in the city?"

I sat up a little straighter. "I don't know. I've got a lot of friends who have been there for a while, and I'm hoping they can help get me some parts in some shows. I've got a pretty good résumé already, but to get the kinds of parts I want, I really need to do more work in New York."

Now, it was my brothers' turns to nod.

Gabe cleared his throat and straightened his pants. "I meant, what are you gonna do for work?"

That was the conversation that I *really* didn't know how to have. I stared at my beer. Tilting my head to the side, I slowly answered, "I'm not really too worried about it. I figure I'll see what happens."

My brothers exchanged a glance. Gabe pulled himself closer to the table, closer to me. He rested his arms around his beer. "You know, Carey," he began, "New York isn't a place where you *see* what happens."

I answered that one with my nod. It was the safest response.

"It's a tough place to live," Seth agreed. My mouth dropped open, and I turned to him. I never expected him to take Gabe's side. Realizing what I was thinking, Seth smoothed his hands down his pants. He chuckled. "It's not Boston, you know. It takes money to live in the city."

My tone grew a little irritated. I didn't mean for it to, it just did. "It takes money to live in Boston, too, Seth, but I've done just fine." Now, if there was one thing I had learned by the time I was four, it was never to give Seth anything that he could perceive as a challenge. And that was exactly what I had just done.

Seth narrowed his eyes and tightened his lips to make the face that he always made right before he hit me when we were kids, but he relaxed quickly. He knew I was frustrated with Gabe. He was always frustrated with Gabe.

It must have been nice for him to see someone else getting grilled by the oldest for a change.

Gabe looked concerned. "Mom and Dad won't be helping you out anymore. You're more than welcome to stay with any of us for a little while, Carey, but not forever."

"I wasn't planning on staying with mom and dad or either of you guys."

They were both shocked at my assertion. Gabe lifted his pint off the table, leaned back into his chair, and took another sip. Seth moved closer to me.

Blinking a few times, Gabe asked, "So where were you planning on staying?"

"With a friend of mine in Brooklyn."

"So you'll be *living* with your friend?"

"For a little while, I guess. Until I get my own place."

"You can't get your own place if you don't work."

"I'm gonna work. I'll probably wait tables or something."

"You can't live in Manhattan these days on a waiter's salary, Carey. I'm sure Seth can tell you that." Gabe turned to Seth who had been distracted by one of the girls in leather standing up at the bar, but as soon as he saw Gabe set his jaw, he came back to our conversation. He nodded. I wondered if he knew what he was agreeing to.

"I was planning on living in Brooklyn anyway," I said.

"Even Brooklyn isn't affordable anymore. Seth can tell you that too."

Seth nodded again.

"Look, Gabe," I was being diplomatic. I could tell that Gabe's concern was turning into frustration. "I know plenty of people who are doing it. Things are tight for them, but they make it work. I can too." I didn't really know how to get myself out of the conversation.

"And what are their lives like?" Gabe *was* getting angry. I'd seen him act like this with Seth when we were younger, but he'd never used this tone of voice with me.

"They do just fine. They're happy."

"Happy that they don't have a future? That they aren't giving anything back to the people who care about them? Carey, you're not a kid anymore. These are the things you have to think about now. You have responsibilities, responsibilities to your family and yourself. Where do you want to be in five years? In ten years?"

What was I supposed to say? I could tell him that I wanted to be an actor, but that wouldn't be a sufficient answer. So I did the one thing I never thought I would ever do in my entire life: I rolled my eyes at Gabe. I didn't mean to. It just happened, and as soon as I did it, I wanted to apologize, but...

"Forget about it." Gabe finished his beer in one gulp. Setting the sudsy glass back on the table, he said, "I'm gonna go to the bathroom." He stood up and stretched. I nodded in the direction he should go, and he sulked away.

I felt bad. I knew he was disappointed in me. He had helped me out a lot with money while I was in school, and I guess he figured that once I got out I'd repay my debt to him by paying something to somebody else. I was going to do that, just in my own way.

As soon as he left, Seth pulled a pack of cigarettes out of his pocket. "I hate the way he looks at me when I smoke," he admitted. After taking one out, he set the pack on the table and nodded to let me know that I could have one. I thanked him, pulled one out, and let him light it for me. The waitress came by again. Seth ordered another round for us.

He grinned as she walked over to the bar. He watched her place our order, and he turned back to me. "Don't let

Gabe get to you," he said. A haze of smoke clouded and dispersed around his face. "He's been pulling that shit with me for forever. 'Why don't you start a family? Why don't you move back out to Jersey?'" With a flick of his wrist and a purse of his lips, Seth waved away everything Gabe had ever said. He laughed. "What do you expect? He's a doctor. It's just the way he is."

I snorted a short laugh, flicked my ash on the floor, and leaned into the wall.

I was glad to be alone with Seth. My guilt was already dripping away. He always stuck up for me. Granted he was the only one who ever got really angry with me, too. But he always told Gabe that I should get to do whatever I wanted to do. Thank God for Seth.

Seth finished his beer. His smile disappeared. He deepened his voice to add, "I am serious about the money, though."

I quickly tensed my body. Seth must have sensed my reaction because he laughed apologetically. "Come on, Carey. Forget about all that shit Gabe said. I'm just talking about you doing what you want to do."

"That is what I want to do, Seth," I whispered.

He threw his hands up in mock surrender. "Okay, okay. Far be it from me to smash your dreams of being a starving artist in the big city." He laughed and leaned closer to me. His dark eyes shined in the dismal light. "But you know it's not the nineteenth century anymore. Hell, this time next year, it won't even be the twentieth century, and if that whole artist thing didn't go out with the invention of capitalism, it definitely ran straight for the door when e-commerce came around." He laughed again. I didn't. "Carey, I'm just saying that you're young. You wanna be able to live. You'll be in New York City. Don't you want to eat at a restaurant instead of scraping change together for a slice of pizza? You should be able to go to clubs and bars that have more attractions than the sixty year old drunk falling out of his chair. I'm not saying that you should give up acting, just get yourself some capital, *then* worry about making art. Christ, if you do things right, you could live off the interest from your investments alone, and with the elasticity that the market has these days, you could retire by the time you're thirty. I'm serious. I know people who do it. Me, I love it too much, but you, you'd have all the time in the world to act. Plus," he pulled his chair closer to me, and he whispered conspiratorially, "You don't wanna have to hustle some little hottie in a cab all the way back to Brooklyn." He laughed again. I couldn't figure out what he thought was so funny. "I mean, Brooklyn might be kind of cool these days, but if you wanna wait tables, you're gonna be living in the ghetto, man. And none of the city's finest wanna bare their sweet stuff in the hood." He raised his eyebrow and nudged my shoulder.

I didn't answer.

Seth leaned back into his chair. "All right. I'm just saying that if you wanna live in New York, then you should *live* in New York…"

"I will be living in New York, Seth, just a different one from the one you live in," I said, and I glared at him.

Seth didn't think there was a New York other than the one he lived in. His smile disappeared. He gave me the look. He leaned towards me, but I didn't cower away from him. I waited to see what he would do or say. We were two grown men in a bar. What was going to happen? Was he going to spit on me? Smack me in the face? Even if he did, for the first time ever, I wasn't scared. I guessed I'd have to spit back at him or maybe even hit him. The bouncers would break us up before Seth hurt me, but I wasn't so sure that Seth could hurt me anymore…

Right then, the waitress brought our beers. Seth had to smile at her as she leaned over the table. "You're lucky," he whispered to me.

I didn't believe him, and I didn't care.

He waved me off as if I'd actually offered to pay, and he pulled a money clip out of his pocket. He counted the bills out slowly, mouthing each amount and glancing up to see if the waitress's eyes lit up at the size of his wad. He gave her a two dollar tip on each beer. She smiled as he handed the money to her. He winked at me. His smile curled wider and wider as he leaned towards her. She pulled the money from his hand, and she walked away.

I was embarrassed.

Seth picked his beer up off the table. He took a sip, but before wiping his lips, he leaned over to mash his half-smoked cigarette out in the ashtray.

I looked up quickly. Gabe had come back. Glaring disappointedly at both of us, he slid back into his seat. I was trembling, but I didn't stop smoking.

He looked at the fresh beer in front of him. "You ordered this for me?"

Seth nodded.

Gabe looked around the bar. Then, he said slowly, "You guys figure anything out while I was gone?"

Seth laughed.

We sat silently for a little while. My brothers were practically ignoring me. Eventually, Gabe asked Seth what he thought the future held for the market. Seth spouted out a few theories about off-the-charts growth and wireless technologies or something like that. I didn't know anything about any of it.

Pretty soon, the second beers began dwindling down to nothing. Gabe said he was going to take off as soon as he was done. Seth said that he should probably head back to the hotel too. They asked me what I was going to do, and I told them that I thought I'd sit at the bar for a little while longer. Gabe nodded politely. Seth didn't even look at me. They picked up their conversation where they'd left off. Pretty soon, they were standing up to leave. Seth murmured something about how goddamn early Boston closed, and they each gave me a hug. But the tension never disappeared.

Once they left, I ordered another beer.

I glanced around the bar. The gay bartender was flirting with some young guy who had come in all alone. An old drunk was unsuccessfully striking up a conversation with the washed-out woman next to him. A group of hipsters on their way to some club were trying to figure out what the best round of shots would be to get them pumped for the evening. The smell of spilled beer and stale smoke and fresh sweat stuck in my head. I inhaled deeply. It smelled nice.

The waitress came back. "You're not leaving with your friends?" she asked.

"They're my brothers," I said.

"Really? You don't look anything like them."

"I know."

I asked her if I could bum a cigarette from her. She smiled at me with a sweeter smile than she ever gave to Seth, but I didn't care like he did, and she pulled a pack out of her pocket and handed me one.

I lit the cigarette with the fat, little candle on the table. Smoke streamed toward the dim lights above everybody's head. My own puff swirled through the air on its own for a bit before mixing in with what everybody else was exhaling. I leaned back into the wall. I could smell the nervousness from my conversation with my brothers sweating through the armpits of my shirt. "I'm through with being Gabe and

Seth onstage," I said. I thought that maybe I should spill some beer so that I could be even more of a piece of everything that was going on around me.

Percival

They went to Providence to get the letters etched into their necks.
It was Kane's idea. He had a friend there. They all had
friends there. Johnny had gotten two machine guns in an X
put on his calf down there. Pauly had gotten the straight
edge crucifixion scene on his back in a little tattoo shop
above some café by the river. The same day Pauly had had
the work on that piece started, Big Lou had gotten another
artist to write "vegan" down his forearm. Matt, in some
sort of Bloodlet-inspired Satan Edge craze had hopped on
the commuter rail one day to get the red inverted star put
on his shoulder. Mark, who everybody called Mork, had the
three uneven Xs – more proof that he really was from Ork
– inked onto the back of his leg at the same shop Kane had
taken them to. But Kane had been in jail with the guy who
put the newest letters across their necks. They'd been
locked up together right before Kane had gone down to
New York four years ago. That was why he'd done it for
free, and that was why Kane had said they should go there.

When Kane had come back to Boston, all the kids
except Matt had remembered him. Big Lou, the oldest
except for Kane himself, had been a 16 year old edge kid
who'd actually hung out with Kane before he'd split. Back
then, Johnny was still just a little punk rocker with pink hair
who hung out at Harvard Square to get away from all the

kids who picked on him at school. Pauly was a skinhead
back in the day. He swore he was a sharpie, but Big Lou
and Johnny remembered him being a nazi. Mork had still
skated and smoked pot, and Matt had never even been to a
show.

The only reason Percy was there was because Maggie
brought him along. She was staying with some punk rock
girls (who had been friends with both her and Johnny
before they'd gone straight edge – before Johnny had hit
another kid they'd all been friends with in the head with a
bike lock), down the street from where Percy lived with his
mom and dad. When he'd worn the tee shirt that day, Percy
was hoping that the white girl with dread locks and an
eyebrow ring and a tribal tattoo around her ankle would
notice him. He was a fifteen year old black kid who was
standing at the bus stop in a pair of loose jeans, shell toe
running shoes, and a black tee shirt with flames on the
front. The back of the shirt preached about how the world
needed a firestorm to purify it. With his hands deep in his
pockets, he was waiting for the bus to take him to Central
Square. Hanging a faded messenger bag over her shoulder,
Maggie walked up to him. She stood next to him, and she
told him that she liked his shirt. "So you're straight edge?"
she asked. For the first time ever when somebody asked
him that, Percy nodded proudly. "I thought you looked
familiar," she said.

Whether or not she remembered him didn't matter. He
definitely remembered her, and he knew the faces of all the
kids in the crew before she even thought about taking him
to the Common to hang out with them.

When Maggie and Percy got there, the Park Street stop
was thronged with people. The dark steps leading up from
where the Red Line fueled the city to where the Green Line

breathed on trolley tracks was a solid mass of bustling bodies, but the over forceful white girl and the excited black kid fought through the crowd of families and tourists and college kids. They shoved their way up the stairs from the subway lines, and eventually, they stepped through the dirt smeared, plexiglass doors to breathe the Common's fresh air.

The sun and the breeze broke upon them. Maggie stopped for a moment just outside the doors. "I thought they'd be here already," she said.

Percy nodded as if he had been thinking the same thing.

"Well," Maggie thought out loud, "Johnny probably won't come. He met this girl who goes to BU," she explained, "And they don't ever leave her dorm room anymore, but Kane and Big Lou said they was gonna come, and Mork and Matt and Pauly was the ones who *wanted* to come here today."

Percy nodded and coolly thrust his hands into his pockets.

"Forget about it. We'll just sit and wait." They walked over and sat down on a short wall right outside the boxy, white concrete subway exit. Maggie kept her eyes glued to the doors they'd just walked out of. Percy's eyes wandered across the people in the little cement square at the edge of the Common. Slowly turning his head to take them all in, he smiled sadly.

Maggie slapped his shoulder, "There they are." Percy's eyes lit up. He spun back to the subway exit.

A guy with shaggy red hair, a shadow of whiskers, and a pointed goatee was just stepping through the doors. Both of his forearms were solid pieces of brilliant colors. He ran his hand through his hair. The dirt in it left it straight. His tee shirt was old and faded and even ripped a little bit along the bottom. His jeans had long paint smears down them.

His tennis shoes were about to fall apart. He was carrying a messenger bag over his shoulder. Once he stepped into the park, he held the door open for the guy who was following, and he looked around for his friends.

The first guy was tall and wiry, but the guy behind him was huge, with thick wrists and even thicker forearms. He was wearing a pair of big, clean khakis. His tee shirt was tucked in so that everybody could see how massive his torso was. His wet, black hair was combed neatly to the side. He was the first one who saw Maggie sitting on the wall. Pointing at her, he slapped the dirty guy's shoulder.

Maggie stood up and waved. Smiling, the dirty guy started walking toward them. The big guy clenched his fists, hunched his shoulders over his chest, and rolled in their direction. A quick shape darted out the doors behind them. In the midst of its blur, it slapped the big guy on the back of his head. The big guy's neatly combed hair fell a little out of place. He snarled and turned around.

The shape behind him turned into a kid with brightly bleached hair and huge camouflage pants. He was leaning back, clapping his hands, and laughing in the big guy's face. The big guy pointed to his head. He reached out to try and slap the smaller kid. The kid blurred again. Slyly scooting underneath the large arm lunging at him, he spun around and boxed the big guy's head one more time. Then, he was leaning against one of the doors to the subway, holding his chest because he was laughing so hard. A girl who was dressed sharply in big pants and a tight tee shirt appeared next to him. The big guy smiled at her. The little guy put his arm around her. The big guy nodded at Maggie again, and all four people – the big guy, the dirty guy, the little guy, and the girl – started talking to each other and walking toward her.

"I didn't think you was gonna come," was the first

thing Maggie said. The little guy gave a jokingly perplexed look and pointed at himself. Slipping out from his girlfriend's arm, he slid up to catch Maggie in a smiling embrace. She lifted her legs off the ground. As the little guy spun her from side to side, Percy noticed the muscles beneath the tattoos on his forearms. He set her back on the ground, stepped away, and the other two guys quickly stepped forward and gave her a hug. When the friends were done saying hello, the other girl nodded and smiled at Maggie. Maggie politely smiled back.

"This is my friend Percy," she said.

The dirty guy nodded his head backward, "What's doin'? I'm Kane."

"I'm Lou," the big guy introduced himself.

"Big Lou," the little guy, who was actually bigger than Percy, just smaller than Lou, added for his friend. He stepped forward to shake Percy's hand. Percy wiped his palms on his jeans. "I'm Johnny," the guy went on, tightening his grip almost to the point where the newcomer's fingers hurt. Without looking away from Percy, he pointed over his shoulder at the girl who was with him, "That's Maria." Maria waved. She had a thin neck and frail features. She looked almost like a dainty version of a super model. Smiling, Percy waved at her. Leaning back, Johnny crossed his arms. "You're straight edge?" he asked.

Before Percy could answer, Maggie broke in, "Of course he is. Why else would I have brought him?"

Slapping Percy on the shoulder, Johnny snorted a short laugh, "Then you got a new crew." Percy smiled from ear to ear. He'd never had an old crew.

"Where's everybody else?" Big Lou asked.

"Mork stayed down in Allston with Pauly and Matt last night." Everybody nodded a little bit. Maggie shaded her eyes. In a tone that was a strange mixture between admiration and admonition, she said, "All right yuz guys, let's see the work."

Slowly and ceremoniously, without dropping his arm from Maria, Johnny turned his head. On the back of his neck, right in the middle, above his tee shirt collar, glistening in the sun, were three letters written in the same script as the *Boston Globe's* title: T.O.L. The freshness of the wound made the black ink look wet. Beneath the archaic shapes, Johnny's skin was raised slightly from the scar of the needle's incision. The intricate forms shined brilliantly in the light, and the straight edge kid's soft, white neck seemed even paler where it met the ink of the gang-style, body graffiti.

Maggie ran her fingers around the tattoo's sharply delineated edge. She whispered, more to herself than to anybody else, "That's wicked cool, Johnny."

"Of course it is," Big Lou broke in, "It was Kane's idea."

Maggie smiled an almost flirtatious smile that seemed a little out of place on her face. Kane smiled back confidently, but she directed her comments to Big Lou, "Let's see yours."

Big Lou's neck was too thick and bulky. Dwarfed by his flesh, the letters seemed somewhat awkward and diminished, but Maggie still admired the work, "Nice." She looked back at Kane, "And you?"

Kane grinned. He was missing a few molars in the back of his mouth. He tilted his head to the side, and he turned it so that Maggie could see his neck. Around the ink lines, freckles dotted his skin. The wound was fresh and new, but the splotches of pigment made it look more ingrained in him. The letters didn't look like a new addition. They looked like something that had always colored him. The tip of a larger, faded tattoo peeked up from beneath his shirt.

Then Kane turned back around. Looking at Percy, he creased then expanded his eyes. The black kid shifted uncomfortably.

"Guess we'll have to take you down and get you one someday too," Kane said from behind a dirty grin.

"What's it mean?" Percy asked, knowing that his parents would never let him back in the house if he had a tattoo.

"Thugs of Liberty," Johnny explained. "Or whatever else you can think of. Like D.M.S. in New York. You'll like it."

Percy nodded. Beneath a light-hearted laugh that rang with nervousness at its edges, Maggie said, "You don't even know him. How do you know he wants one?"

"He's straight edge," Big Lou said, "He's gotta have some work."

"Or go to jail," Johnny laughed and glanced back at Kane. Kane rubbed the back of his neck and smiled.

Maggie shook her head, "Sometimes yuz guys are so retarded."

Percy grinned and took it all in. He'd seen all the kids before at the few shows he'd been to. No matter who was playing, whether the band was from Boston or New York, or somewhere down south or out west, Kane always helped them set up the drum set. He always crouched down on the side of the stage and surveyed the crowd that was so much younger than him. He would smile and nod with the music. He would glance around angrily if a fight ever started to break out on the floor, and if it didn't stop on its own, he would fly down from the stage, and one of the kids would wind up in a headlock or on the ground or out the door.

But Johnny was the first person who distinguished himself from all the other kids with big pants and tattoos and shaved or bleached or dreadlocked hair. It was Percy's first show. The shy, black kid was standing at the back of the tightly packed, sweat scented club. The band was walking around on stage, tuning their instruments, smacking and tightening the drums. The vocalist was talking to some kids who were leaning against the stage until he finally glanced over his shoulder and saw that everybody was ready. He stood up. On the barely elevated stage, his lanky, tattoo riddled body was a thousand feet tall. He said the band's name. After a four count on the high hat, the guitars crunched and the drums smashed and the vocalist screamed. The whole place went insane.

Some kid inadvertently drove his elbow into Percy's chest. Clutching at his lungs, Percy stumbled backward. The dark club was a whirling mass of arms and feet and heads. Fingers were raised high in the air, pointing at the stage. The band was rocking back and forth violently to the music. The vocalist was shouting and pointing at the crowd. His body was contorted in some sort of vengeful agony. His eyes were wide. The kids' voices echoed his every word.

Suddenly, the music's speed turned into a rhythmic chugging. That was when Percy first saw Johnny. He was a buoy that couldn't be drowned. He was a kid with bleached blond hair leaping on top of the writhing crowd. Beneath him, his peers' hands and heads were shifting and unsteady, but Johnny walked smoothly from one end of the club to the other. Just a shadow blocking pieces of the bright stage, he punched at the human floor in an enraged rhythm. Singing along, he pointed at himself. The vocalist dropped the mic from his hand. Covering his tormented face, he stumbled backward. A group of kids scrambled onto the stage to grab the fallen mouthpiece, to shout the words that the band mouthed. Johnny stopped on the middle of the crowd. The swirling pit was solid beneath him. He spread his arms, and he leaned his head back. The music was silent for a brief moment, and Johnny, in unison with every other kid there, screamed a short phrase about the sins of the world and how they weren't buying in.

Then the racket sped up. It drowned the voices in its rage. Johnny fell through the roaring crowd to land in the middle of the pit. Percy leaned into the wall. Staring at what the music he loved was doing to people, he smiled at what Johnny had just done, and he swore that someday he'd be the kid standing on top of the crowd.

"About time they got here," Maggie whispered. Three more kids walked over to the little group that was waiting for them.

"Percy, this is Mork and Matt and Pauly," Maggie introduced them. The three new arrivals nodded their heads back and said, "What's doin'?"

Unlike the other two, Pauly had dark hair and dark features. He was the shortest but the solidest. His shoulders were broad. His knuckles were broken. A silver spike pierced his face between his bottom lip and his chin. A tiny tuft of dark hair grew around it and led into a chin-strap beard. Matt was thin and taller and handsome. His skin was smooth. His features were sharp. A ring was fixed in his lip. He was wearing a tee shirt that proudly said, "Straight Edge means I'm better than you." He went straight over to Johnny, and the two of them started talking about stereos and graffiti. Mork's nose was a little too small for his face, his eyes were a little too big, and when he nodded at the new kid, a diabolical grin touched his lips. He clicked his tongue ring against his teeth. A slice was missing from his ear. All three of them had work stringing down their forearms, and all three of them had the same three letters emblazoned on the back of their necks.

Kane sat down next to Percy. The newcomer nervously rubbed the back of his bare neck and watched the forcefully kind way in which the friends talked with each other and laughed at each other. Their interaction was the same as the music they listened to, and the lonely kid wanted to be able to make fun of Mork, and to talk to Johnny about graffiti, and to ask Kane about some band that he was too young to have seen. He wanted to be able to mumble and complain with Big Lou and Pauly about the guy whose cigarette smoke they could smell. He wanted Maggie to admire the work on the back of his neck. He wanted a girlfriend like Maria. He needed somebody other than the distant voices on the records to remind him that he was living the way he should.

"Percy, come on, we're goin' for a walk." Maggie waved her arm for him to follow them. Kane stood up, slapped Percy's shoulder, and jerked his thumb for them to follow everybody else down the crowded cement paths leading further into the park.

"So when we gonna take you down to Providence?" Kane asked.

Percy looked at him. Turning Kane's head into a bright silhouette, the sun drove through the trees. Percy squinted and asked, "What?"

"To get you some work," Johnny said over his shoulder. Then, Maria whispered something to him, and he laughed. He leaned closer to her, stumbling just a little as their legs knocked together.

"Will yuz guys forget about it," Maggie shouted from the front of the group where she was walking and talking with Matt, "He doesn't need any tattoos."

Percy thought about saying something, but he wasn't quite sure what it should be. So he just put his hands in his pockets, turned to the ground, and stepped along next to Kane at the end of the line. He glanced up every once in a while when Johnny's sharp laughter broke through the crew's murmuring voices. Sometimes, he cocked his head to the side to watch Kane add a matter-of-fact opinion to whatever conversation was going on. Laughing about where the hell they were going, Maggie and Matt stopped walking for a little bit.

"We're goin' to the Garden," Kane said. The TOL crew followed him as he stepped off the cement and onto a patch of open grass. Mork danced some sort of marionette waltz as he talked and laughed and made a fool of himself. Trailing along just a little bit behind everybody else, Percy disappeared into his own thoughts.

In an instant, someone to his left shouted something about watching where the fuck he was going. Before he could even look up, with a jarring crash, a running body smashed into him. The guy who had hit him jumped up as quickly as he had fallen. "Jesus, kid, what the fuck is your problem?"

Holding his aching head and trying to catch his lost breath, Percy lay still and shocked. Above him, a red face that he'd never seen before sweat and thundered and breathed heavily. The body for the face was long and muscular and slick with sweat. "I said, what the fuck is your problem? Why don't you watch where you're going?"

"Why don't you watch where *you're* fuckin' goin'?" somebody else shouted. Percy glanced up to see Johnny making his way toward the incident. The rest of the crew was standing tensely. Without taking his fixed stare off the shirtless guy, Johnny helped Percy back to his feet.

"I told him to get out of the way," the guy panted between deep breaths.

Two other guys, both half naked and sweating, walked up behind the shirtless guy. One was tall, well over six feet, and skinny. He was clutching a football to his long chest. The other guy was short. He had arms the size of Percy's entire body, and a head that was easily twice as thick. "Yeah, it's not our fault the kid wasn't paying attention," the big-headed guy said.

Shielding Percy with his arm, Johnny stepped closer to the big-headed guy. "It's not *his* fault *you* weren't."

The big-headed guy broadened his back and thrust out his chest and puffed up his neck. He breathed quietly, "Look, if you got a problem, we can solve it." Trying to make their two presences add up to something more intimidating, the skinny guy stepped in closer to his friend. The shirtless guy who hit Percy wiped the sweat from his face and nervously glanced over his shoulder. Two long legged girls were sitting on a blanket with a cooler on it. They were talking sporadically to each other, and they were gazing intently at what was going on.

Johnny's eyes twitched in that direction. He slapped the back of his neck. Watching one of the distant girls raise a beer can to her lips, he stood still for a second. Just as his fists clenched, a lanky, dirty hand grabbed his shoulder. Kane pulled Johnny back a little bit, and he stepped closer without getting too close. The rest of the crew followed. Maggie put her arm around Percy and asked if he was all right. Maria wrapped her arms around Johnny's waist. She whispered something in his ear and kissed him on the cheek. Big Lou spread his arms and lowered his head and glared at the jocks from beneath his forehead. Smiling eerily, Pauly rubbed one hand's knuckles into the other. Standing behind him, Matt crossed his arms. Happily grinning at the action, Mork clicked his tongue ring against his front teeth.

"Yuz guys say it's all right, then it's all right," Kane said.

The big-headed guy puffed up a little more. He flexed his back and pushed his thick arms out even farther than they fell naturally. "Your boy doesn't seem to wanna make things all right," he said, and he nodded at Johnny. The skinny guy crossed his arms. Licking his lips like he could taste the flavor of something he thought he should say, the original shirtless guy moved a little closer to his friends.

Kane laughed a little bit, "He never wants to make things all right. I'm just tryin' to keep everything okay." Kane put his hand out for the big-headed guy to shake.

The skinny guy grinned a silly grin and leaned down to whisper something to the big-headed guy. The big-headed guy snorted a short laugh, "Everything's all right, then, but I'm not shaking your hand." Johnny hardened his face. He pulled Maria's hand off his waist. A slight tremor passed over her features, but she didn't try grabbing hold of him again. She just let her arms dangle limply at her sides.

Kane looked down and laughed again, "How much yuz guys had to drink today? Cuz I can smell the beer on your breath."

"Enough," the skinny guy answered.

Johnny stepped forward. Casting a freezing glance, Kane quickly swiveled around to glare at him before he turned back to the big-headed guy. Maggie stepped away from Percy. Nodding her head toward where they'd come from, she whispered something to Maria. Soon, the two girls started walking away from what was happening. Percy nervously watched them head back to the cement walkway. For a moment, his legs trembled because he wanted to follow, but he knew he couldn't. So he just tried to glare, not too menacingly, at the three shirtless football players on the Common.

"Looks like your girlfriends got the right idea," the skinny guy said. The original shirtless guy turned albino and looked like he might vomit. Kane shrugged.

"Yeah, why don't you follow them back to where they keep the trash," the big-headed guy said.

Kane put his hand to his ear. "What's that?" he asked. Slipping his bag off his shoulder, he stepped back and laughed. He started turning back in the direction they'd come from. Percy began breathing a little easier, but everybody else stepped up a little closer to the jocks.

Still smiling, and just shaking his head almost unbelievingly, Kane stepped away. The big-headed guy relaxed his impressive shoulders a little bit. He chuckled to his friends, "Fuckin' freaks with their white-trash girlfriends protectin' a—"

With a thud, Kane's bag hit the ground. Before the big-headed guy stopped talking, the redhead's dirty, mangled fist smashed into his jaw. With a crack and a whip, the guy's thick head jerked back on his over-sized neck as if the hand of God had taken that moment to grab him by the hair. His eyes rolled into his skull. The bottom half of his face stayed a little out of place. He wobbled a bit. Then his knees buckled. Stumbling, he bent over to spit out a thick trail of red and a blood-stained tooth.

"Get 'im Billy!" the skinny guy shouted. His eyes lit up, and he stepped back from his friend's fight, but before Billy could regain his balance, Johnny kicked him underneath the chin. There was another crack. Billy's face snapped back up. With his fat head lolling on his thick neck, he collapsed to his knees and then to the ground.

With a dull smack, Mork stomped once on the back of Billy's head, burying half of his glassy face in the grass and the dirt. "What the fuck!" the skinny guy screamed. He grabbed Mork by his bony shoulders, but before he could do whatever he thought he was going to do with him, Big Lou slammed one of his huge fists into the back of his head. The skinny guy spun around and swung wildly. He actually tagged Big Lou, but Johnny kicked him in the knee, and when he stumbled, Big Lou wrapped one of his hands around his face and threw him backward. He landed on the ground. Mork started kicking him in the ribs, and Johnny kicked him in the side of the head.

The original shirtless guy whispered, "Oh my God." He turned to run, but he'd only taken a couple of steps before Matt was able to catch him and throw him to the ground so that Pauly could stomp on his face and his neck and his shoulders and his groin. He just cried, "Leave me alone! God, will you fucking leave me alone!" but once Matt started kicking him too, he ran out of breath. He closed his eyes. The only sounds were the dull thuds of their feet slamming into his curled up, half naked body and Pauly shouting, "Shoulda watched where you was goin'!"

One of the long-legged girls who had been sitting on the blanket had disappeared. Percy had watched as both of their faces contorted when Kane hit Billy. They jumped up and started talking to each other when Johnny kicked him. By the time Big Lou hit the skinny guy in the back of the head, one girl was running and the other one was holding her cheeks and shaking her head and nervously staring past all the action. Percy turned to look back down the path they had come up. What he saw was enough to make him stop breathing.

Coming through the park, pumping their arms and breathing heavily, were three cops. Faces went blank as people turned their heads at the Marathon. Percy licked his lips and ran his hand down his face. Shuffling from one foot to the other, he thought about shouting something to what was now his crew, but he didn't know what to say.

Pauly was the first one who noticed the cops. He stopped kicking the guy who was crying and shaking on the ground. "RUN!" he shouted, and he took off through the Common. Being the closest to Pauly, Matt was the next to look back over his shoulder. He leaped overtop the wounded shape beneath him. Mork and Lou and Johnny and Kane were animals disturbed from a meal. Panting, they looked up with blood-crazed expressions. Mork smiled and almost laughed. He kicked the skinny guy one last time in the leg. He bumped into Big Lou, grabbed his shoulder, and ran off in the opposite direction from Matt and Pauly. Tripping, Big Lou turned around. He caught himself, and he thundered off, close behind Mork.

Johnny and Kane looked at each other. Kane narrowed his eyes back to sanity from their Manson-like expression. He leaned over and picked up his bag. Johnny raised his shoulders and pointed at Percy standing alone. Percy glanced behind himself. Two of the cops had broken off. One was running after Mork and Big Lou. The other was going after Matt and Pauly. The last cop had his walkie-talkie in his hand. Red-faced and sweating, he was shouting something as he ran on.

Then they were off. Johnny grabbed Percy so quickly that he almost tumbled from the force, but he quickly recovered himself. Soon, he was running, neck and neck with his two new friends.

They ran straight at the cop. Just when it looked like they might meet him, they turned a little. In his solid, thick soled dress shoes, the cop slipped on the grass. A divot flew into the air, and the cop fell down.

The three of them ran into a quickly parting crowd of people. They dodged around and leaped over the bodies and the benches and the sculpture. They skirted through three lanes of honking traffic. Cops were coming at them from both sides. Their blue shirts were billowing around their bodies pushing against the breeze. Their badges were glinting sparks of the sun. They were pumping their arms and straining their faces.

The straight edge kids hit rough cobblestones. Buildings

loomed above them. They were dashing through hundreds of shoppers and tourists.

Before Percy knew it, they'd reached Downtown Crossing. Johnny shoved him into the subway stop. Their feet echoed across the crowd between the white walls. They ran to the turnstiles. Kane was the first to put his hands on either side of him and lift his legs up and over. Johnny used one hand as a pivot. Percy did the same as Kane. Someone yelled, but the edge kids didn't stop running. They followed Kane down the steps to where the subway screamed through the city's bowels.

"Hope I guessed right," Kane panted as they tried blending in with everybody else who was waiting to hear the Red Line scream through the tunnel. Percy was shaking. His thoughts were running even faster than he had just been. Every once in a while, he glanced at Johnny whipping his sweating face in every direction or at Kane running his fingers through his goatee and staring down the dark tracks and whispering, "Come on, come on…"

A roar and a screech of brakes bellowed down the line. With a rush of wind, the train slowed to a halt right in front of them. The doors swished open. Piling in with all the other people, they sat down and waited for the train to seal itself off so that they could leave.

Kane relaxed and tried making himself more comfortable in his pleather chair. Johnny leaned forward and wiped his hands down his face. Percy was still shaking and sitting taut and rigid. Screeching around turns and casting flickers of blue sparks outside the windows, the train barreled through the city's belly. Kane glanced at his knuckles. He rubbed them against his other hand.

"I can't fuckin' believe those guys," Johnny whispered. His arms were shaking, but not out of nervousness like Percy's, his were shaking in anger. "They think we're gonna be scared of them."

The train rumbled on through the tunnels. Kane laughed a little. Percy grinned, but his eyes stayed wide and terrified.

"They think they can say somethin' to one of us without sayin' somethin' to the rest of us. They don't know what it means to be friends," Johnny went on. "Fuck them," he spat, "If it were up to me, I'd kill every one of 'em." He raised one of his hands up like he was holding a gun, and he squeezed off one shot, two shots, three shots. The guy sitting across from them looked up at the ceiling and rolled his eyes toward the window. He looked everywhere but at Johnny.

"Where'd everybody else go?" Percy wondered.

Johnny shrugged. He didn't care. "We'll find 'em," Kane calmly answered. "Get off at Central?" he asked. Johnny nodded, but he didn't loosen his angrily tightened eyes.

The dark tunnel lit up again. Screeching, the train braked. Percy looked out the window to see the familiar, colored tiles decorating Central Square's arched walls.

"That's why I thought you were right when you said we should get the work," Johnny said as they stepped onto the platform. "That way everybody knows we look out for each other. Me, you," he slapped Kane's chest, "Big Lou, Pauly, Mork, Matt. You too," he turned to Percy, "That's why we gotta take you down to Providence. Edge kids gotta stick together."

Percy nodded. Kane draped his arm over Johnny's shoulder. He shook him back and forth.

"Maggie doesn't always get that," Johnny whispered. "She thinks she can still be friends with everybody else." Trudging back into the sunlight, he let his voice trail away.

People were everywhere. They were stopping by the

stores, drinking iced coffees, and sitting on the benches. The three edge kids walked down the street. The traffic went by them. The people went by them. Percy kept glancing over his shoulder for cops, but Johnny and Kane seemed to have forgotten about everything that had happened on the Common other than what Billy had said right before Kane had hit him. "I'm just sick of people fuckin' with me," Johnny kept saying, "I'm fuckin' sick of it," he said as he refused to move for the people going past. Kane smirked and nodded.

Then Johnny stopped walking. "What the fuck you lookin' at?" Percy heard him say. He whipped his head back around from looking over his shoulder so that he could see who Johnny was talking to now.

Some skinny, white kid, who was about Percy's age, dressed all in black, with shaggy, pink hair and a wristband of spikes juxtaposing his frail features and his timid expression, was sitting on a bench smoking a cigarette. At Johnny's words, he looked behind him to see who the kid with the bleached hair and the tattoos was messing with. When he realized that there was no one there, he turned back around. He flipped his wrists out like, *I don't know*, and he shook his head. He took another drag off his cigarette.

"Hey, I'm talkin' to you," Johnny shouted. He strutted up to the kid. In a quick motion, he slapped the cigarette from the kid's hand. With a rain of sparks, it hit the ground. The confused kid looked up at Johnny.

"I... I wasn't looking at you," he mumbled.

"Sure didn't seem that way, huh?" Johnny said. He glanced over his shoulder at Kane, who, glaring at the kid, shook his head in agreement.

Exhaling sadly, the kid turned his face to the ground. Percy bit his lips and rolled his eyes. Johnny leaned down to breathe onto the back of the kid's neck, "You lie to me again, and I'm gonna break your fuckin' neck. Now, what were you lookin' at?"

Slowly raising his head, the kid sounded like his mouth was going dry, "I swear I wasn't looking at you."

Johnny leaned back and clapped his hands, "For somebody who wants to look like a tough guy, you sure don't act like it," he laughed. He squatted down to the kid's level. "I'll tell you what, though, just for wanting to look so tough, I think the three of us oughta take you out." The kid raised his eyebrows in a sort of questioning fear. Kane smiled from above Johnny. Just so that he wouldn't have to see the expression on the kid's face, Percy mashed an already mangled cigarette butt even more.

"Look, I… I really didn't…"

"But you know what, I'm gonna give you a choice." Johnny leaned forward a little bit. Quickly gazing into the street, the kid fidgeted his fingers. "If you admit you're a bitch, then we're not gonna touch you."

The kid turned back to Johnny. He gazed into the straight edge kid's stone-like features. The little punk rocker looked like he might get sick. "Whaddaya… Whaddaya mean?"

Scratching the tattoo on the back of his neck, Johnny smiled, "I mean, you say you're a bitch, and we won't touch you. Otherwise, I'm gonna crack your fuckin' skull right here."

Kane smiled a little, "He will, too, you know. I'd like to stop him, but I don't think I'm fast enough."

Percy ran his sweaty palms down his legs.

The kid looked at the ground. He mumbled something.

"What was that?" Johnny said. Cupping his hand around his ear, he leaned forward to spit his words across the kid's neck, "What did you say?"

The kid mumbled something again.

Johnny straightened up. "You know what," he said, "I'm gonna count to three, and if I don't hear you say, 'I'm a bitch,' I swear to whatever God there may be that I'll scrape your fuckin' face down the pavement and bury you in the sewer. One, two…"

"I'm a bitch," the kid said. With tears forming in the side of his eyes and spittle catching in the corners of his lips, he pleaded with Johnny, "Okay?"

Percy knew that if he had to keep staring at the look on the punk rocker's face, then he was going to get sick. So he turned around to check for cops.

"All right," Johnny said. For the first time since they'd left the Common, he smiled the friendly smile that he'd had when he'd introduced himself to Percy. "Let's go back to my mom's and see where everybody else is at."

Johnny headed off. Laughing and patting his friend on the shoulder, Kane walked right beside him. Percy stared for a little bit at the kid's downturned head and humiliated posture. "Come on!" Johnny shouted. A hurt look bled through his eyes, but Percy slowly wandered away to catch up with his new crew.

Cream

When Stephen crossed through the traffic flowing down the Damrak, he looked over his shoulder to see Jack and Eileen still sitting together on the patio of one of Amsterdam's coffee shops. Stephen had been sitting on that patio with them, relishing the scent of the hash they were smoking and quietly watching his friend flirt with the girl who was staying in their hostel with them. He'd told them he was going to go to bed. Eileen had asked him to stay. Jack had smiled at him. And Stephen had decided to go back to their room. But when he'd lain down to write in his journal, the thumping bass from the club beneath his floor intruded on his thoughts. Stephen threw his pen into the binding of his open journal, put his clothes back on, and left the dingy hostel room to wander the city to find something that he wasn't sure what it was. But he was in Amsterdam, and that meant that he could find anything. Sometimes anything is better than something.

Reaching the other side of the Damrak, Stephen set one foot on the curb. In the near distance in front of him, the streets and alleys glowed red. The frightfully happy sound of what must have been a million murmuring and screaming voices swirled through the air. Stephen pulled a crumpled pack of cigarettes out of his pocket. He stuck one between his lips, lit it, and inhaled deeply. The smoke tasted light and clean.

Stepping through his tobacco puff, Stephen was engulfed by a perpetual procession of drunken, shouting men mellowed here and there by a few high, giggling women. The endless parade accepted him into their midst, and soon Stephen was crossing over a canal, rounding a corner for his first glimpse of the district.

The cobblestone street that he was looking down was flanked on either side by two and three story row houses. A long canal flowed down the middle. People leaned drunkenly against the railing or walked along with the water. They stared up at the glass fronts and glass doors of the houses. Above each door, an orbicular bulb hung. Some were black, but most glowed as red as the embroidery adorning a black kimono, outlining a serpentine dragon. It reflected in the water and draped its shade across the gawking bodies. It lit the cobblestones and bounced from them back to the buildings where it swam brilliantly on a pulled shade or died in a pale reflection on a white lit window.

Behind the windows, dancing in the reflection of a thousand red lights and a million staring faces, were the bodies. From a distance, every woman was a gyrating, sliding form of leather or lace on flesh. They were thin and muscular, fleshy and fresh, still and seductive, loose and beckoning. They danced in basement dungeons, stared out of second floor cages, and blew kisses from street level cells. Their hair whipped around their necks. Their hands caressed the glass. Stephen stepped into the crowd between the buildings.

To his right and to his left, drunken Asians and Europeans and Americans stumbled and sneered and jeered at the women. Doors opened, and men either grinned and hid their faces or proudly stepped into the embraces reaching out from the glass. Sometimes a man would step out from the door, brush off his clothes while staring at the ground, and melt into the crowd before anybody else had a chance to say anything to him. The red light would click off, and a disinterested woman would appear in the bright window. Stephen stared at it all.

A girl in black lingerie was standing behind one of the windows. She smiled through the glass at Stephen, and Stephen stopped walking to smile back. Her face was narrow and triangular. She had high cheekbones and an upper lip that curled up and around her teeth like the top of a Valentine heart. When her long lashes were open, her eyes were the brightest blue. Her hair was black, and its waves crashed over her shoulders. "Come here," she mouthed to him from between her red lips. Her long, painted nails ensnared him and dragged him closer. The crowd parted around him. He stepped up to her door. Enamored by the milky flesh that curved out around and beneath her lace, he reached out to touch the glass, but before his fingers rested on its cold surface, the prostitute opened the door.

She put one long leg into the street. Her heel clicked on the cobblestone. Stephen followed that sound up her firm calves to the smooth thigh that she was rubbing. She smelled like jasmines.

"What is your name?" the English words rolled off her tongue's thick accent.

"Stephen," he answered numbly.

"What do you want, Stephen?"

"I – I don't know."

"Thirty-five guilder, and you can have anything," she cooed as she reached out to rub her hand down his shoulder.

He shivered beneath her firm caress, "I don't have any money."

Stepping back into her room, she laughed, "Then go get some and come back." She closed the door to her smiling face. For a moment, Stephen stared past his reflection at her. His chest ached. His throat felt heavy. He could have cried as the fragrance of her presence disappeared to be replaced by the shouts in the night air. Merging back into the crowd, he put his hands back in his pockets.

That was the most beautiful woman I've ever seen, he thought. He tried imagining what he could have done to her, but nothing too creative came to mind. He just wanted to stare at her forever.

He kept walking. Above him, in a second floor window, another girl propped her stiletto heel up on a chair. She drew a whip across her thigh and rubbed it beneath the leather skirt she wore. Her face was angular and painful. Her eyes were harsh and seductive. Stephen was sure to look away before her gaze brought him toward her.

To his right, there was an alleyway where the crowd thinned out. Stephen glanced down it. A group of four kids a little bit older than Stephen stood in the muted glow outside one of the doors. Suddenly, the door opened. A pale light lit the opposite wall. One kid, smiling and lost, stumbled out of the brightness back into the maroon tinted alley. His friends laughed and slapped him on the shoulder. Another one of them ventured inside. The door closed again, and the light above it burned through the darkness. The kids outside laughed and playfully slapped each other. One of them stepped closer to the door and jumped up and down while shaking his head from side to side like he was getting ready for a boxing match. One of his friends came up and threw his arm around him, "Hurry up, man!" he yelled at the door. "We ain't got all night!" He turned, met Stephen's eye, and winked. Not knowing what to do, Stephen walked away.

He flowed along with the crowd into another cobblestone street. This one was narrower than the first.

A sharply dressed man stepped out of a black, wooden door. His black, button down shirt was stiff, and his black jeans were tight. His pointed boots clicked on the steps leading down from the door. He stared at Stephen. He started speaking with the slight trace of a vague accent. "Live sex show for you, my friend. Two girls, one guy, only seventy-five guilder for a ticket." The man smiled, revealing his bright, white teeth.

"I don't have any money, man," Stephen apologized.

The man in black laughed. He ran his fingers through his goatee. "No money? What is wrong with you? The free market and you don't have any money. Listen, my friend," he said, and he straightened up, very business-like, "There is a money machine if you go to the end of the street and turn right. Then take your first left and go to the end and turn around the corner to the right. Get some money, and I will sell you a ticket for seventy guilder."

Stephen grinned sheepishly.

"Come on, what is your problem? This is the best show in the red light. I will tell you something. There is a girl in there," he jerked his thumb over his shoulder. Smelling of whiskey and cologne, he stepped closer to Stephen, and he whispered in his ear, "With thighs so strong she can push a fucking dildo back out of her cunt. I swear, you will cream in your pants. It is the best investment that you can make in Amsterdam. After this, you do not need to spend any more money tonight." He laughed and slapped Stephen on the shoulder.

With his mouth and his eyes open wide, Stephen slowly backed away from the man in black. He put his hands in his pockets, spun away from the salesman, and started walking quickly, his legs brushing together as if he had somewhere important to go, in the direction the man was pointing. "The free market," he whispered to himself over and over again.

When he got to the end of the street, he turned right. Then, he took his first left. The crowd was thinning out, and Stephen followed the brick building around a corner to the right.

He fumbled below his pants' line for the money belt around his waist. Slowly, he drew out his ATM card. He slipped it into the machine. Drawing the card the rest of the way into itself, the mechanical device sounded a rattling sigh. A blur of numbers and directions came up on the screen. Stephen poked and prodded the beast until it gave him what he wanted...

When he rounded the corner in the other direction, Stephen had a hundred guilder nestled between his fingers in his pocket. Ruffling the corner of each paper rectangle, he tickled the small wad of bills with his thumbnail. The sweat from his palm moistened the textured paper, making the money stick to his hand. Merging back into the crowd, Stephen was stone-like and purposeful. Once again, the crowd carried him along their tracks as he first turned right this time, then left, to walk back down the red glowing alleyways, to nimbly and carefully pick his way between the bodies staring out of their glass cages.

In the bustle, the man in black was still standing at the foot of his club, hawking his wares to potential customers, offering deals to the men, the women, and the couples, telling them the glorious things they would be able to see if they would give him the money he was asking for. He smiled at Stephen, and he opened his arms as if for an embrace. The lights shimmered off his shirt's slick fabric. "Come back to see the sights!" he exclaimed, "It can be a beautiful world, my friend," and he swung his arm to usher

Stephen toward the door, "Seventy-five guilder if you have it now."

Not even acknowledging the dark, towering presence, Stephen walked past the man.

"But don't you want the girls?" the man laughed and shouted at Stephen. The American's hunched shoulders disappeared among the whistling crowd.

He walked down the same street that he had first come up. He carefully looked in all the windows on his left. There were black girls and white girls and Asian girls in leather and animal prints and bikinis and lingerie. They were sitting and staring and pointing and smiling. Purposefully gazing at each girl, Stephen kept walking, continuing before any of them asked him to come closer. Tinting everything their seductive color, the red lights glowed across the crowd.

Stephen stopped so quickly that the couple behind him, with a foreign grumble, had to drop hands and skirt around his immobile frame. As he stared at the girl in the black lingerie, with her black hair tumbling over her shoulders and her blue eyes open wide above her high cheeks, he smiled. She opened her red, heart shaped lips to smile back.

The cobblestones beneath him were as ethereal as the glow in the night air engulfing him. Glancing around, Stephen licked his lips and shifted his weight from one foot to the other. The prostitute's smile grew larger. Stephen stepped up to her door.

Pulling open her see-through cage, the prostitute melted through the air. She ran one hand up the length of the doorjamb, and her molten shape solidified against it. She cocked her head against her raised arm. The wooden frame liquefied and filled in the gaps around her heat. She curled her tongue and cheeks and slid them around her words, "Thirty-five guilder for a suck and fuck."

Shivering even though the night was hotter than hell,

Stephen nodded. He didn't say anything. He was too worried that the sounds would never make it out between his chattering teeth.

Accentuating her heart-shaped mouth, the prostitute's smile grew even larger. She slid her gaze down Stephen's throat and tickled his insides. Moving aside, she let him into her room. In her high-heels, the four inch lifts of which shaped the muscles in her calves, she was a full head taller than the American. Sliding past her, he could feel warmth radiating from her taut flesh. He could smell the lilac-like fragrance of her world. She switched on the red light. The cobblestones beneath her window glowed. A new reflection appeared in the canal. Closing the glass door, she pulled down a black shade so that nobody outside could see what they were going to do to each other inside.

With white walls and a white ceiling and a white tile floor, her chamber was immaculately sterile. An unfinished wooden dresser stood against the wall with a mirror and a sink next to it and a little stereo on top of that. The bed was across from the sink. With thick pillows and piled sheets, it was nice and comfortable and high. A glossy poster of a woman with her legs spread wide and her head tilted back in ecstasy was on the wall above it. At the head, on a flat table that took the place of a headboard, was an assortment of sex toys. Dildos of all shapes and sizes were placed in a neat row in the very back. In front of them were condoms and oils and creams and beads and whips and gags and harnesses and things that Stephen wasn't even sure what to do with.

"Money?" she asked.

Standing in the middle of the room, Stephen turned to her, "What?"

"Money," she said again. She put out her hand to

receive the bills.

"Oh… Oh yeah," Stephen mumbled. He reached into his pocket, pulled out the crumpled wad, and peeled off two notes.

"For one hundred you can stay for one half of an hour."

With two bills already dangling from his extended fingers, Stephen froze. His heart was beating a deep, rhythmic bass through his chest. The scent in the air was choking him. His thoughts were cloudy, but the world was still clear.

The prostitute smiled and stepped closer. Her heels clicked across the linoleum. Reaching Stephen, she bent down to his ear. Her hair tickled his cheek. Its dark strands spilled over his shoulder to warm his back and rest on his chest. A light purr slipped through her lips. She ran her long hands around his waist to end with one hand cupped between his thighs. Stephen rose onto his tiptoes. Her grasp followed. She whispered, "What would you do to me for that time?" She glanced at the toys behind her bed. Stephen swallowed slowly. He stuffed all of his sticky, balled up money into her free hand.

Carefully straightening out each bill for counting, she grinned and walked back to the wooden dresser. She slipped the money into a slit on the top. One at a time, the bills slid from her hand into the wooden holding cell.

"What is your name?" she asked in between mouthing the amount that each additional note added up to.

"Stephen," he answered, "And you…"

"Where are you from?"

"America."

She nodded.

"What's your name?" he asked.

Without looking up, she answered, "Mona."

Stephen rolled his eyes to the ceiling. "That's a very nice name," he said.

"Thank you," Mona said. She turned around. "Take off your clothes and lie down on the bed."

Stepping out of his shoes, Stephen unbuckled his pants and slid the loose jeans down his thin legs. The pale, hairless sticks made his face turn red. He slipped his shirt off his smooth, lanky torso, and he wished that he had muscles to flex. "Underwear too?" he asked.

"You are not at the doctor's," Mona laughed.

Stephen pulled down his boxers. Quickly turning around, he walked over to the bed and sat down on the edge. A plastic sheet covered the spread. It stuck to his pale, bony flesh. Trying to keep his knees locked together, Stephen scooted around uncomfortably.

"You are American," Mona said, "Do you like Wu-Tang Clan? They are American."

"I don't really listen to them," he answered.

"I like Wu-Tang Clan," she said. She stepped over to the stereo on the sink. She pressed a couple of buttons. A few quick words were blurted through the speakers, and a rhythmic beat expanded into the air. A New York accent, drenched in slang, reacted to the rhythm. Letting the sound course through his body, Stephen leaned into the wall to rest his head below the poster above the bed.

Following the beat, Mona walked up to him. She swayed her round hips at every echoing click of her heels. Nervously licking his lips, Stephen ran his hands through his shaggy hair.

When she reached him, Mona lightly pressed his shoulder to move him around and lie him down on the plastic bed covering.

She sat down in front of him. Reaching her fingers between her breasts, she grasped the clasp to her bra.

Twitching her nails, she undid the snap. The little piece of lace slipped down her back, spilled through the air, and fell to the floor. Nothing in her body's shape changed without the bra. Her breasts were still perfectly full. Even Stephen knew they were fake, but nothing about Mona was real. "You touch everything except the pussy," she said.

Brushing her breasts against his forehead, Mona leaned overtop of Stephen to grab a condom. With her long nails, she slid the tiny piece of latex onto him. She leaned forward to settle her head between his legs.

Stephen tried to relax. He wanted to touch Mona, to run his fingers through her hair, to press his palms against her flesh, but he couldn't. With his gaze, he traced the curves of Mona's body. The muscles in her shoulders sloped up and down to the motion of her head. Her back was firm and straight. Her waist slid out into her hips. One of her strong, shapely, pin-up legs lay straight behind her on the bed. The other, waving in the air, was bent at the knee. With the straps of her heels clinging to her milky flesh, she rocked her calf back and forth to the music.

His own spindly limbs were tensed against the plastic sheet. Swallowing, he closed his eyes. The image of his unenticing form buried beneath the prostitute's perfection was burned into the darkness behind his eyelids. His face twisted. A spasm passed through his body, and he relaxed.

"Stop Mona," he whispered. When the slight sensation of her teeth through the condom didn't stop, he spoke a little louder, "Mona, please stop."

Mona turned her head up. "You are done?" she asked.

Stephen reddened. His stomach turned. He glanced at the ceiling. "Yeah, but I... I want to know where you're from."

"What?"

"I wanna know where you're from."

"Why does it matter?"

"Because I like your accent."

"Prague. I come from Prague," she answered. Crawling up Stephen's thighs, she whispered, "You would like something else soon?"

"I don't know. Maybe in a little while."

Mona shifted around on the bed. Her body heat rose off of Stephen's legs. "Okay," she said, "It is your money."

Stephen turned away from the ceiling. With a smile at the edge of her lips, Mona was staring at him. He quickly looked away. She laughed, "This is your first time with a woman?"

Stephen opened his mouth a little. His face turned even redder than it had been before. He stammered. "No. No, it's not."

"You are sure?"

"Yeah," he nodded, "I'm sure."

"It is okay if it is."

"It isn't."

"Okay," Mona said. Then, she wondered out loud, "How old are you?"

"Eighteen," Stephen answered, still without looking at her. He glanced around the room, but there was nothing for him to look at. The walls were empty. The dresser was bare. The only things that added any color were the poster above him and the toys behind him, and he didn't feel like looking at either of those. His stomach was relaxing, but he still wasn't comfortable. "It doesn't make any sense to me," he whispered.

"What?" Mona asked, leaning toward him.

"This," Stephen said, "It doesn't make any sense."

Mona shrugged.

"I mean, what you do makes sense. That's just supply

and demand, but why guys wanna do this. That doesn't make any sense."

"You like it," Mona answered. She leaned over the side of the bed and grabbed Stephen's boxers off the floor. "Here," she said as she tossed them to him. Catching them, Stephen carefully slipped the condom off. Mona handed him a trashcan and some paper towels that were beside the bed. Without looking at what was in the yellow basket, Stephen dropped the rubber into it. He wiped himself off, threw away the paper towel and quickly scooted into his underpants. Poised on the edge of the sheets, Mona stayed topless.

Enriching every word with her accent's flavor, she started talking distractedly. "Some men come to me because there are things that they want that their girlfriend or wife will not do, or there are things that they want that they do not want their girlfriend or wife to do. They are looking for a fantasy." Mona stood up. She started walking over to the sink. "And some men come to me because they want me. They do not know what is real so they waste their money on nothing."

Stephen watched her long legs cross in front of each other as she stepped. He wanted to ask her why he had come to her, which kind of person he was, but he was too embarrassed to find out.

When Mona reached the sink, she pulled a drawer open, pulled out a pack of cigarettes, stuck one between her lips, and lit it. After a quick exhale, she turned off the music. Glancing at Stephen through the haze fogging the mirror, she explained, "It does not fit anymore."

"We can smoke in here?" Stephen asked, but before Mona nodded, he was reaching to the floor for his jeans. Rattling the buckle, he settled back into the bed and lit a cigarette for himself.

Carrying an ashtray in her hand, Mona walked back to Stephen. She sat down and set the ashtray between them for them to share.

After a drag, Stephen asked, "What do you think of the guys who come in here?"

Mona pursed her lips. Stuck out like that, they looked even more like the shape on a Valentine's card. She shrugged, "I do not think anything." Pausing, she passed her hand straight down in front of her face and chest, tracing a wall. "Nothing," she added.

Stephen nodded. He glanced around the room again. It was as empty as it had been before. He turned back to Mona.

"Why do you do this then?" he asked.

Mona shrugged. "I know," she said.

Stephen nodded. He thought that he had asked too much.

They were silent for a little while, just sitting there, watching each other inhale and exhale smoke.

It's all a bit more real, Stephen smiled to himself.

Mona laughed. "You have a very nice smile," she told him.

Stephen put out the cigarette. He let the smile stretch through his cheeks.

"It is nice when a person will smile with their whole face," Mona said.

"What?"

"Many people, when they smile, they smile only with their lips. You smile with your whole face. That is why I invited you in."

"Why you invited me in?"

"Yes. Some men, when I look at them, and I smile, they smile only with their lips. I will not let them in. When you smile, it is in your eyes." Mona reached over to run her long fingernails down Stephen's forehead, past his lashes, to his cheeks. It made him feel warm inside. "You smile with your whole face. It means that you are not lying to me. You are a nice person."

"Thanks," Stephen mumbled. He pulled away from Mona's caress. He didn't know what to say.

"Yes. You are nice. You are sure this is not your first time?" she asked again.

"I'm sure," Stephen answered. He stared at the plastic covering the bed sheets. Without looking up, he asked, in a soft voice, "Why do you only let in people who smile with their whole face?"

"Because when I was younger I had a problem."

Stephen answered with a knowing nod of his head.

"Yes." Mona scooted one leg beneath herself. "When I first came here from Prague, a man came to see me. He was very tall, and he wore all black, and he made me very uncomfortable, but I was very young, and I was very poor, and I needed every customer. I tried to smile at him because I knew that if he smiled at me, it would make me relax, and I could make him happy. Have you ever watched somebody smile at you with only their mouth, when the rest of their face stays nothing?" Stephen thought for a moment, but he wasn't sure if he had ever paid enough attention to anybody to know. He shook his head. "It makes a smile emptier than any other way a person can look at you.

"But I was very young back then, and I did not want to lose a customer, so I let the man inside. He told me to get undressed, and I did. He told me that he wanted to watch me with myself, and I did that too. He told me to close my eyes, and I did because I was young. I could hear him moving around my room. He whispered about 'dream girls'. I could feel him come closer to me, but I tried to relax and to make my money. I thought that soon he would want me to touch him, and I could make him happy, and he would leave. But you cannot make somebody who cannot smile happy.

"I could feel him breathing on my face, and I could feel his hands near me, but he would not touch me until he grabbed my hair. I opened my eyes, and he pulled a razor out of his pocket. He yelled something about me not being real, but that he would make me just like everybody else, he would cut me one time for every dream that he had lost that night. He started to slice me right here." Mona spread her legs a little to let Stephen see a faint scar that stretched from the inside of her thigh up to her underwear.

"I screamed louder than the rest of Amsterdam that night. All of the other girls in the house ran in from that door." She pointed to a door that Stephen hadn't noticed the whole time he had been in the room. It was in the wall behind her head. The monochromatic paint on it made it look like it was a piece of the never-ending white walls. "They pulled him off of me, and they called the police to take him to jail."

"Jesus," Stephen breathed heavily. "At least you're all right."

"Yes," Mona nodded slowly. Her gaze glassed over. Bringing herself back to the room she was in, she glanced at the stereo on her sink, and she added, "There is not much time left. Do you want anything else?"

"No," Stephen answered, shaking his head, "I think I'm just gonna go."

"Okay," Mona smiled. "You are very nice."

"Thanks," Stephen said. He stood up to step into his jeans. As he glanced around the room again, a funny sensation, different from the one he had felt earlier, tickled his stomach. Quickly covering his body, he bit his lip and shook his head. Mona stood up as well. She put her bra back on. She grabbed Stephen's hand and led him back to the door.

They were standing behind her chamber's pulled shade. "Thank you," she said.

"Yeah," Stephen answered, "Thanks."

Mona opened the door. As Stephen went to step out, she grabbed him and pulled him close to her warm body. "Come see me again," she whispered into his ear, warming his face with her breath.

"Definitely."

She pressed her lips against his cheek, and she let him go.

Stephen stepped back into the night. The door closed behind him. For a second, he was able to drink in the red light's rich luster on his skin. *I guess that was all right,* he thought. His grin stretched all the way into his eyes. *Yeah, I did all right.* Then, the glow was gone. Stephen stared at his pale hands traced by the bright light shining out the door behind him. The stench of piss replaced the aroma of flowers.

A toothless old man burst out of the crowd. In a foreign language, he said something to Stephen. Smelling of liquor, laughing like they were old chums and pointing at Mona's door, he embraced Stephen.

The laugh wrinkles at the edge of Stephen's eyes disappeared. He smiled back with his lips. The old man shook him heartily by the shoulders. Stephen kept grinning, but when the old man began walking away from him, still shouting something in a foreign language and still gazing longingly at the closed door, Stephen's smile disappeared completely. He walked away without a single backwards glance at Mona.

After a few steps, he began kicking a pebble that was

near his feet. He followed its scuttling path until he finally booted it into the water. Watching the little rock tumble through the air to disappear beneath the reflecting canal's black surface, he snorted a mirthless laugh. He ran his hand down his face. His stomach opened up and spilled an aborted thought into the canal. In his mind, he pictured Jack and Eileen curled up together in one of the small beds in their hostel. He thrust his hands into his pockets. "I got nothing," he whispered to the anonymous crowd carousing through the glowing night. "Nothing." Digging deeper into his pockets, he turned around to wander back through Amsterdam's maze-like corridors.

Mitch and Michelle

"Oh God, will you please hurry up," Mitch whispered into the chilly November air. With the words, a mild mist of breath rose off of his lips. When he was a little kid and that used to happen, he would move his fingers up and pretend he was smoking a cigarette, but he wasn't a kid anymore. His breath disappeared before he noticed it.

He anxiously tapped his fingers on the rock he was sitting on. The rapids roared all around him. They raged in an overlap of white water that consumed itself quicker than it consumed everything else, but for now, Mitch was safe and dry on the rock.

The bank across from him was stark and lifeless. In a vain attempt to puncture the low-lying, gray clouds to let the sun stream through to warm the world, the leafless trees reached their naked limbs into the sky, but the clouds were bunched too closely together. The branches clattered in a bone-like rattle beneath the wind's breath.

Mitch was so far away from it that every gust was a dying man's sigh. "I'd rather be over there," he mumbled, but he couldn't get there. His side of the rock dropped into nothing other than the rapids. He'd gone as far as he could. The path was on the other side.

Turning a little, he looked over his shoulder at where he had come from. The wind had streaked his wet footprints across the stone surface, but they still held their beaded shape enough to tell that they had come from him. Farther away, a few steps from where he had clambered up from the river's lower rocks, Michelle was carefully picking her way along the jagged path.

She was walking on water. In the wind, her hair streamed off to one side. Trying to figure out where to go from every step, she paused and shook her head. The desolate bank behind her was no different from the one across from Mitch, but she was a splotch of reality on the dismal scene. The color of her clothes and the curves of her body added a dimension to the world. Her slow motion invigorated the frigid landscape. Mitch spun back around and tried burying his face in his sweatshirt's neck.

She stamped her feet behind him on the rock. "That last step was almost impossible," she said. "The water was rushing across it so fast I almost asked you to come back to the other side with me."

Mitch nodded slowly.

Michelle's damp tennis shoes squeaked as she came closer to him. Mitch brought his shoulders up and tried disappearing into himself before she got there, but there was nowhere for him to go.

Michelle was standing and shivering next to him. He didn't look up at her. He knew how she was looking down at him. It would be the same way she had looked at him after he had kissed her when he had gotten off the train. She tilted her head to the side, knit her eyebrows together, and pursed her lips. Mitch thought she was so beautiful when she looked like that, when she was studying or thinking about something serious, but that was before. He had been gone a long time, much longer than the time had actually been.

Exhaling heavily, Michelle sat down next to him. He

didn't look at her. He didn't think he could. He wasn't sure what would happen if he did.

She bumped her shoulder against his. "So what's up?" she asked.

Mitch gazed out at where they couldn't get to. He shook his head and mumbled, "Nothin'."

"Somethin' must be up," Michelle went on. "You've been actin' like a freak ever since I picked you up."

Mitch shrugged and fiddled with the folds in his jeans.

"All right," Michelle said. For the first time, she sounded a little annoyed.

With each of them sitting on their own little piece of the rock, thinking their own private thoughts, and wishing that something about right then could be different, they were silent for a little while.

Finally, Mitch stammered, "I met somebody else."

He didn't look at Michelle when he said it, but he could feel her lean toward the water. He could sense her tighten her jaw as her stomach twisted into a knot. He knew that her mouth was drying out and her eyes were filling with tears because the same things were happening to him.

"I figured that," she mumbled.

He looked at her. "Why didn't you say anything then?" he asked.

"What was I supposed to say? I figured if you wanted to tell me, you would, and you did." She turned away from Mitch and stared down the path the rapids were flowing along. She sniffled, raised her shoulders, caught them, and slowly dropped them. "So what do you wanna do now?" she asked.

"I don't know," he answered. "I guess we should break up."

Michelle nodded, "If that's what you want." The wind carried her voice away to drown it beneath the rapids.

"You don't think we should?"

Michelle turned back around. Her eyes were almost ready to overflow. She was looking in her boyfriend's direction, but she wasn't looking at him. "I think it's up to you," she said.

"Why's it up to me?"

"Because you're the one who met somebody else."

Mitch looked down at the rock. He shook his head. "I can't make that choice."

"You have to. It's not mine to make. I still love you."

"Even after this?"

"It doesn't change the way I feel. It just hurts."

"If it was the other way around, I'd break up with you."

"I know. But it's not that way. It's this way."

Mitch dropped his head into his hands. *Why won't you just break up with me?* he thought. "I don't know, Michelle. I just don't know."

Michelle nodded. Her voice cracked as she spoke, "Well, call me when you figure it out." She stood up to leave.

Without raising his head, Mitch reached up and grabbed her arm. Her thick sweater trapped her body heat. Her skin couldn't warm his wind-blasted hand. "Please don't go away," he begged. Tightening his fingers, he added, "Not yet."

Michelle stood still for a second. Mitch listened to the rapids. She sat back down. He let go of her. It was nice to know she was still there.

They didn't look at each other. They didn't say anything to each other. Feeling the distance widen between them because the distance shouldn't have been there at all, they sat there.

Mitch shifted around a little. He looked up at the sky. "I didn't expect you to say that," he said.

"What did you expect?"

"I don't know."

"You figured I'd cry and ask you why?"

Mitch shook his head, *No*, but that was a lie.

"Or you figured I'd yell at you and leave you alone?"

Mitch shook his head, but he was still lying.

"I thought you knew me better than that by now."

"I do," Mitch mumbled.

"You think I didn't know something like this would happen? I mean, you're meeting new people all the time..."

"It's not like I *met* somebody new. I just kinda hooked up with this girl. That's all."

Michelle straightened up. She looked at him with that expression that he had always thought was so beautiful. "Then why'd you tell me about it?"

"I don't know. I just figured you should know."

"That I should know or that I should break up with you?"

Mitch raised one shoulder to show that he didn't know the answer.

Michelle slouched down. She drooped her head. "So *you* wanna break up?" she asked weakly.

Mitch didn't move.

"You wanna break up with me for some girl you don't even know."

"I didn't say that."

"What did you say then? Will you please just tell me something?"

"I don't know. I didn't think it would be this hard."

"To get me to break up with you? I've waited for you for two months. Because I thought you were worth it. I *still* think you're worth it."

Mitch burst into a flurry of nervous motion. He started looking around frantically for something to throw into the river – a twig, a pebble, a scrap of paper, anything that would break the endless surface of white noise – but there was nothing there other than him and Michelle. "Jesus! Will you just leave me alone!"

Michelle jumped up. She was trembling. Her face was twitching. "What are you gonna do?" she asked hesitantly.

"I'll figure it out," Mitch whispered as he dropped his head into his palms.

"I don't know what the hell is wrong with you," Michelle said. She turned around and started walking away. Mitch didn't try to stop her this time. She might have been crying.

He was alone in the middle of the river. In the distance, Michelle's car crunched through the gravel parking lot and zoomed down the winding road that led back to both of their homes. Mitch kept sitting there.

His mind wandered back to the other night, to a drunken party, and to Cora. He thought about how soft her short, dark hair was. Still smelling her Japanese perfume's aroma, he inhaled deeply. He grinned at the recollection of her small body's smooth curves winding around his.

"That was worth it," he whispered. "That was what I wanted."

His grin spread up his cheeks to crinkle his eyes. Snorting a short laugh, he looked back down at the river. The memory warmed him enough that he didn't feel the wind's bite.

As he sat there feeling pleased with himself, the evening's bright colors began bleeding through the gray day. The air's texture changed. The clouds took on the rich luster of a fall night. Beneath the sky's elastic clarity, the bank across from him transformed. The wind picked up. It sent its fingers to prod through his clothes to try and touch his bones. He shivered.

He started trying to figure out how he was going to get home now that Michelle was gone. Thinking about that reminded him of his parents, of saying goodbye to them when they dropped him off at college. He remembered saying goodbye to Michelle as well. He remembered kissing her in his driveway. He held her close as tears trickled out of the corners of her eyes. He had cried too, but not until after she was gone. When she was still standing there, he had buried his face in her hair's pleasant smell.

"I missed you so much, Michelle," he whispered to nothing and to nobody.

He traced his fingers along the rock. The creases in his skin got caught on the jagged surface as memory after memory, things he hadn't thought about at all over the past two months, washed over him.

He remembered the time when Michelle's parents had gone out of town. He'd stayed at her house that weekend. One night, he'd laid a comforter down for them to lie on to watch a movie. He'd smoothed it across the hardwood floor. He'd pushed down every ripple in the fabric so that they could lie on something soft. Michelle had stood above him the whole time. He'd felt her there, watching over him, and he'd felt something inside himself. As he spread that blanket across the floor, he'd realized that he'd found something, some sort of security that steadied him. He was completely in love with Michelle, and he never wanted that to end.

"That was stupid," Mitch whispered to the empty night descending upon the river. The wind answered with a gust that rattled the trees into a chorus sounding like cicadas. Mitch hugged himself tightly. It was almost completely dark now.

He ran his fingers across the contours of his face. His bone structure felt hollower than it ever had before. "She should be home by now," he whispered. "And if she isn't, she will be by the time I get somewhere to call her," he told himself. "And then I can talk to her, and I can fix all this."

Nodding his head, he stood up. He turned around distractedly and walked to the other side of the rock, but when he got there, he froze.

The last step, the one that Michelle had complained about, was gone. Searching the river, hoping that, in the darkness, he had simply misplaced his memory, Mitch turned around frantically, but the rock wasn't there. Nothing other than the river, dark now beneath the darker sky, surrounded him.

"The tide must have risen," he whispered. The rock beneath him didn't feel solid anymore. The river that constantly raged against it, chipping away at it, had finally dissolved it into itself. Numbed from vertigo, scared he might fall, Mitch sat down. "I'm stuck," he admitted. "I'll be stuck out here all night."

It would get cold, too, colder than he was certain he could live through. He wouldn't be able to sleep. If he did, alone in his sweatshirt, he might freeze. He would have to stay up at least until the first hints of day peeked through the clouds, and even then, he might still be stuck for hours. The loneliness of his thoughts and his feelings might drive him insane. His parents would be terrified. "What did I do?" he wondered.

A dark, waterlogged branch, battered by and drowning in the waves, floated past him. "Jesus, what the hell am I doing out here?" he wondered. Nobody answered. He started to cry.

The Storyteller

Halfway through their trip, Dan and T stopped in a cemetery. Casting flickers of light on the worn and faded tombstones, the sun sliced through the trees. The grass was long and tall and prickly when the two travelers sat down in it. Dan pulled a pipe and a plastic bag out of his pocket. He took the bud out of the bag, spread the bag across his lap, and began to methodically break apart and pick through the weed.

The world was a little hazy that afternoon. T closed his eyes and decided to wait until his mind was clear before opening them again. He leaned into the lop-sided tombstone behind them. His skin was sticky and salty from sleeping all morning and sweating onto the upholstery of the little VW Bug that the two of them had driven down there in. The sun felt nice though. Its warmth was refreshing, and its light was invigorating.

With the click of a lighter, the scent of thick, green smoke swirled into T's nostrils. Dan tapped his arm. Without opening his eyes, T raised his hand to take the bowl. He stuck the pipe between his lips. The smoke filled his lungs and his stomach and his shoulders. He exhaled and grabbed the lighter to take another hit. Breathing the smoke out slowly, he drooped his head and handed the bowl back to his friend.

Using its heat to solder his broken synapses, the weed was working through T's mind. He opened his eyes.

In front of him, beneath the shadow of a hanging willow, was a lanky shape. Passing through the light and the dark, the shape shifted and stepped closer.

It was a boy who was no older than fifteen. Hanging down to his chin, his stringy, bowl-cut hair wisped over his zit-encrusted pores. His shoulders were hunched. The sweatshirt covering him was loose and hanging. His jeans, which were at least a 50 inch waist roped down to fit all 25 of his, were frayed along the bottom. Everything about him, from his emaciated build to his decrepit clothes to his awkward gait, gave him the appearance of being a walking resident of the cemetery.

Dan coughed violently. The wanna-be-hip hillbilly smiled a dirty grin. "Can I get a hit?" he drawled.

T glanced at Dan who glanced back at him. Dan raised his shoulders. T nodded. Leaning forward, Dan held the bowl out to the kid.

The kid sat down across from the two travelers. With a polite nod, he took the little, glass bowl gingerly between his thumb and forefinger. He grinned a little, chuckled a little, sparked a lighter that he produced from his pocket, and he took a hit.

Dan and T were mesmerized by his absurd presence. He took another hit and passed the pipe to T.

"Where y'all from?" the kid asked.

"Jersey," T answered.

"What're y'all doin' down here?"

"Driving."

"Long drive," the kid noticed.

T nodded.

"So what're y'all's names?"

Dan was lost. T had to answer for both of them.

"That your real name?" the kid wondered.

"No. My name's Vietnamese. Nobody can say it. They just call me by the first letter," T answered. He put the pipe back between his lips.

"Yeah, I'm like that too. I mean, ev'r'body can say my name. They just don't. They call me somethin' differ'nt."

"What do they call you?" Dan asked.

The kid bowed his head, and he shook his dirty hair. "It doe'n't really make sense anymore. It ain't true. It's what people use to call me, and it stuck."

"What is it?"

"They call me the Virgin."

Dan and T both nodded knowingly. The Virgin grinned.

The three of them went on sitting in a circle, in front of the tombstone, on top of the grave, until the bowl was done. Then, Dan packed up another one.

The Virgin was handing the pipe over to T, nodding to let him know there was a little left. His lungs were puffed up with smoke. The two travelers could hear its fumes in his voice when he huffed, "I know where we could get some acid."

T left the bowl floating in the air in front of his mouth. He cocked his head to the side. Licking his lips, Dan leaned forward.

"Yeah, I do," the Virgin laughed. "Just what we need."

"Let's do it," Dan said. He glanced over at T who killed the bowl in one long toke.

T found himself in a parking lot. He didn't know where he was. "How did I get here?" he asked the sky.

Above him, the stars poked bright holes into the night. The moon burned down to be consumed by the brightness of the streetlights. Everything beyond the sparkling asphalt was blackness and nothing. It had been a good trip so far.

"Come here," T heard somebody say. Looking around him, he discovered that the Virgin had disappeared. Dan was standing in a shadow at the edge of the lot. Entranced by the glittering road of broken glass leading up to his friend, T walked over to him.

He bumped into Dan before he realized he should stop walking.

"Where are we?" T asked.

"I don't know. Maybe he could tell you."

Looking up, T saw what held Dan captivated.

A stream of water sprayed up from the earth and fell down in a mist. A two foot high stone wall surrounded the pond that it created, making a little walled city out of the pool's inhabitants. With rabbits on their backs, a herd of black deer waded into the water. Ebony frogs sat still on lily pads scattered across the water's surface. Licking their lips, a pack of sleek and powerful wolves twined through the animals. Both the predators and the prey were oblivious to each other. They were entranced by a man seated before them on the other side of the spigot.

The man was darker than the night. He sat in a throne rising out of the water. In one hand, he held a long staff. On top of the staff, at a summit well above the rest of the world, a bird was perched, ready to take flight. The fingers of his other hand caressed the pages of a book that was open in his lap. The beard on his chin pointed to where he was reading. He had taken a break to survey the multitude that was enraptured by his words. His furry animal face was heavy with his knowledge. His eyes grew in an expression of his anger. His long, straight horns sliced into the sky to point at the stars. Even though he had the body of a man, he had the head of a goat.

The Virgin appeared from behind the goat. He walked

around the fountain.

"It's the Storyteller," he said. "I use to talk to him when my mom brought me to church."

"Where are we?" T wondered.

"The Storyteller knows," the Virgin giggled. "He could say your name, too."

"Where's the church?" Dan asked.

"Right behind it."

T didn't see it. He was stuck staring at the way the water shined where it fell on the animals. In those scattered spots, it brought vitality to their iron skins.

"Let's go," the Virgin drawled.

Dan agreed, and the two of them started walking around the fountain.

T remained as immobile and enraptured as the animals.

"You coming?" Dan asked.

T shook his head and stepped closer to the fountain.

The Storyteller was staring at him. His beady eyes pulled him in. The black orbs flashed beneath the moon.

"What can you tell me?" T wondered.

The Storyteller didn't answer. With a blank expression, he stared at the world. Dan and the Virgin had disappeared.

T moved up to the fountain's edge. "We're all alone," he whispered. "You can talk to me now."

The Storyteller didn't answer.

T licked his lips. He wasn't sure what to do.

The fountain pulsed. Like a pane of opaque glass, it rippled out around the lily pads and the wolves and the deer and the legs of the Storyteller's throne to melt into an impenetrable solid. As black as the sky, it didn't seem like there was anything beneath it. It ended and began with the animals rising out of it.

Then, T heard the glass shatter. He didn't see it. He only heard it, but he saw the stars and the moon catch pieces of the broken shards as they slipped along on top of the flowing solid.

T smiled. The Storyteller glared back at him. Beneath the moon, his gaze was as bright as the sun. Its heat brought the morning's sticky sweat back out on T's skin. His clothing itched. He began scratching his arms and his back and his shoulders and his neck.

Twisting and writhing in the darkness on the black world, he pulled his shirt over his head and off. He stepped out of his shoes and whipped his socks off. He slid his jeans and his boxers down his legs and kicked them far away.

Naked and hairless beneath the lights and the moon, still scratching at the salt on his skin, he stepped into the fountain. As his foot broke the surface tension, a coolness coursed through his toes to his heel to his calf to his knee. He smiled. The Storyteller's gaze cooled.

The moon reflected broken slivers on the pool's surface. In the distance, T could hear the world's heart beat. It sounded like the pitter-patter of running feet.

T waded toward the water gushing out of the center of the earth. The slick glass slid around his legs. He thought that it should be cutting him, but it didn't. It flowed around him like water.

In the middle of the fountain, the earth's clear blood pulsed. T stuck his fingers beneath the spray. It tingled on his skin, dripped into his pores, and filled him, washing him from the inside out. The world's heart beat louder.

T closed his eyes and stuck his head under the fountain. The world's blood felt so clean. It was the perfect thing to cleanse his travels' grime off of his skin.

As the cool spray beat down into his ears, he heard the world's heart stop, but its blood still flowed.

Finally, the Storyteller spoke to him. He spoke in a

drawl that was reminiscent of the strange state that T had found himself in. "What're you doin', man?" he asked.

"I was just thinking the same thing," T answered.

"We gotta go," the Storyteller told him.

"I know, but where?"

"It doe'n't matter. We broke a window."

"I know. I'll follow you."

The earth's heart started beating again. T opened his eyes. All of the animals were staring at him. The frogs were entranced. The deer were confused. The rabbits were encouraging, and the wolves were grinning.

T swallowed slowly. His saliva was sticky. It coated his mouth and lumped in his throat. He slid his hands down his smooth skin.

The animals were too stunned to say anything, but the world's clear blood had cleaned them as well.

T straightened up. He could feel the Storyteller's eyes on his back. The earth's pulse faded farther and farther away.

"I'm T," he said.

His audience responded with blank, unrecognizing stares.

"That's not my real name. It's what people call me. Nobody can say my real name." The bunny rabbits twitched their noses. "Except the Storyteller." The frogs crouched down to jump. "I bet that's what he's reading." The bucks lowered their heads. "He's telling us all our names…" The fur on the wolves' backs bristled.

"My name is…" The words caught in his throat. His face twisted. "My name is…" Struggling to form the words, he turned around and dropped to his knees.

Casting his shadow across the traveler, the Storyteller loomed over him. The bird on top of the staff held its wings spread to fly away. The goat's eyes were wide. His face was drawn. His horns pointed at the moon. The world's heartbeat had disappeared, but its blood still gushed. It sprinkled across T's back.

On his knees, T crawled over to his newfound friend. The glass broke around him. Painlessly, it cut his flesh, but T swam through the blood. He hugged the Storyteller's legs.

"All I wanted to do was tell them my name." He raised his head to plead with the bearded goat above him. "But it's been so long since anybody said it that even I can't remember it anymore. Can you read it to me?"

The Storyteller was silent.

In the distance, the world began to cry. It was a mild mourning. At the sound, T's eyes filled with tears. The Storyteller wouldn't even look at him anymore.

"Can you please read me a story?" T asked. "Read me the story you were telling before I got here."

The world's cry grew louder.

"Please tell me something," T begged. The world howled its answer. It wailed so loudly that it spun T's head with its ferocious sadness.

As he sat there, curled around the beast's calves, T thought that he might join the melancholy. He closed his eyes.

Suddenly, the world's cries were so sharp that they split T's mind in half. He couldn't remember his name. He couldn't remember who he was. He couldn't remember where he had come from. And he couldn't remember how he had gotten to where he was at.

His eyes popped open. He saw that the fountain's clear blood was now pulsing crimson. The pool he was in was no longer the dark coolness that it had been. It burned with a bright intensity. T's stomach dropped.

Shouting something unintelligible, he jumped up. The

Storyteller didn't say anything. But T knew it was all in the book that was open on its lap.

He leaned down to read the words. The pages were blank and empty. T fought to turn the pages, but they wouldn't move. The book was blank.

"Why are you doing this to me!" he shouted. He slipped and fell through the glass. Shards sliced him and flew into the air. Trying to breathe, T choked and coughed in the pool forming around him. Trapped under the glass, he was drowning. He punched through the surface and arose drenched.

The earth cried so loudly that it was deafening. T could feel the slick sheen of his own blood coating him. The pool, the animals, the beast, the bird stuck on the staff, even the night had turned red. The entire world was inside out. T wondered whether or not it would ever be right again. Joining his own voice to the world's cries, he screamed.

Something grabbed his waist. He was dragged, kicking and screaming, from the fountain. He yelled and shouted and cursed at the demon holding him.

He face slammed into something. Something was trying to pull his arms off of him. He yelled again, and his captor spun him around.

A huge, hideous man with a torturer's club raised above his head was inches from his face. His eyes were wide and spittle flew off his lips when he shouted, "You make another goddamn sound, and I'll crack your skull."

T looked over the demon's shoulder. Finally, he saw the church. It rose white between the Storyteller's horns. The moon lit it with an ivory glow, but there was one spot, in the middle of a tapestry of stained glass windows, where a black hole had swallowed the translucence.

T screamed. The cop pushed him face down into the

bleeding ground.

Portrait by Pamela Adams

About the Author

Michael Anthony Adams, Jr. is originally from Whittier, CA. He holds a master's degree in Philosophy from the New School for Social Research in New York City. As a teenager, he was the lead vocalist and lyricist for Richmond, VA-based hardcore band Broken Chains of Segregation. In 2012, he began publishing his collected works under the pen name Israfel Sivad. He's the founder of Ursprung Collective, a spoken word/music project referred to as "fantastic brain food" on ReverbNation. He was the primary lyricist on indie rock group One & the Many's first two albums, *Forms* and *Hours*. His writing has appeared in the *Santa Fe Literary Review, The Stray Branch, Badlands Literary Journal,* and more. He currently lives with his partner and collaborator, artist PJ Adams, and their children in Baltimore, MD.

www.MichaelAnthonyAdamsJr.com